SAINT CODE
CONSTABLE

A  NOVEL

SAINT CODE CONSTABLE

A LUCKY DEVIL NOVEL

MEGAN MACKIE

Constable
Book 2 of Saint Code
Copyright © 2024 Megan Mackie. All rights reserved.

Cover by J. Caleb Clark
Typesetting by Autumn Skye
Editors: Laura Mita

Library of Congress Control Number: 2023946720

Paperback ISBN-13: 978-1-965097-25-0
Hardcover ISBN-13: 978-1-965097-26-7
Ebook ISBN-13: 978-1-965097-24-3

To Cierra, my sister-author

TABLE OF CONTENTS

SAINT CODE: CONSTABLE

ACKNOWLEDGEMENTS:

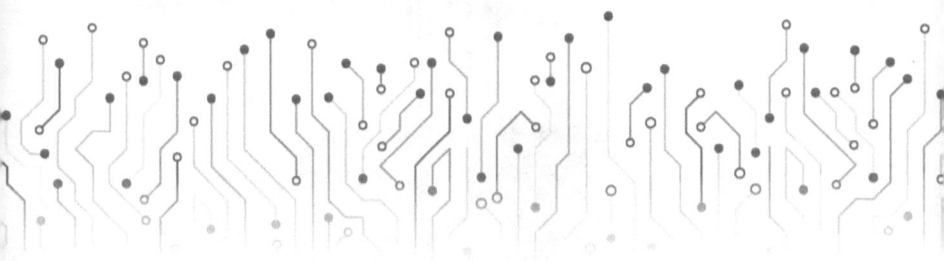

Thank you to my family and friends who support me every day and encourage me to follow my dreams.
Thank you to everyone at 4 Horsemen Publications.

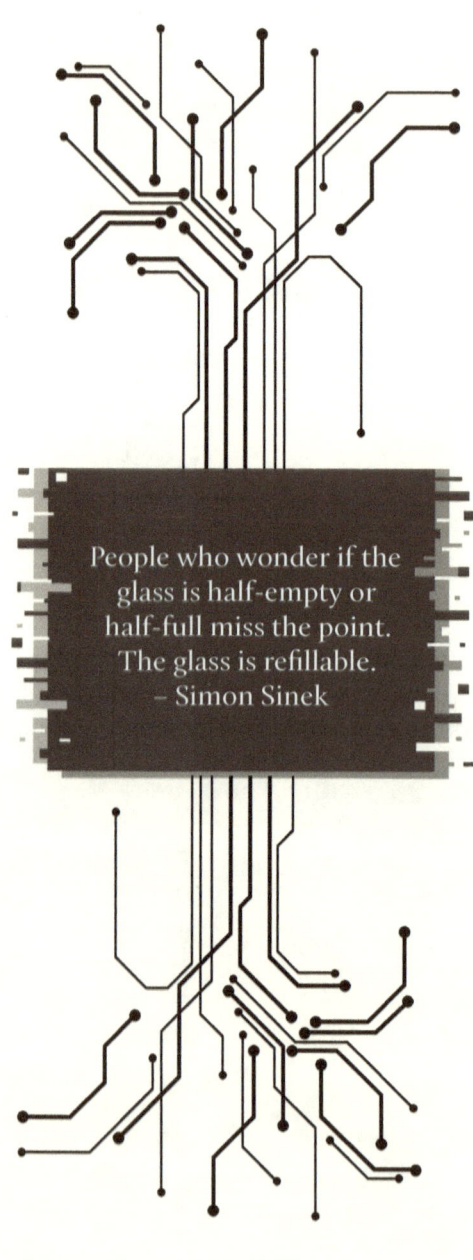

People who wonder if the glass is half-empty or half-full miss the point. The glass is refillable.
– Simon Sinek

CHAPTER I

St. Augustina expected that the job would be hard some days. There would be traumas and sadness. She knew she would see some dark things all in the name of seeking justice.

She just had hoped it wouldn't be her first case.

When she stepped into the two-bedroom Chicago apartment, she thought it could have been the set of a horror movie. Blood had splattered everywhere across the wood flooring, telling the story of how the victim, a woman in her mid-twenties, had fought for her life up until the very last. Her attacker had repeatedly cut her until she'd bled out. From the trail of blood, it was clear she had tried to escape from her bedroom to the front door. The pictures on the wall emphasized the tragedy, full of smiling faces of family and friends beaming, oblivious to their loss.

The body itself was covered by a black sheet, while crime scene techs documented everything with pictures and copious notes. Their faces were grim lines of determination and deep indentations of weariness between their eyebrows. Police

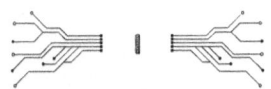

secured the scene, each one with hands and feet wrapped in plastic so as not to corrupt it. The backs of their plastic blazers displayed their acronyms to declare their jurisdiction, and they all spoke in soft, funeral-level voices.

No one acknowledged St. Augustina as she entered. Her nondescript long coat and professional attire along with the badge on a chain around her neck ascribed to her the right to be present symbolically, if not in truth. She bore no acronyms though.

But she wasn't there for the victim; she was there on behalf of the murderer. The purpose of her visit that day was to establish a claim of jurisdiction to this tragedy.

"Hey, who are you?" a voice finally asked after St. Augustina stood watching the techs and the scene for too long.

The voice belonged to a middle-aged man with skin the same soft, warm brown as her own, who obviously loved gumshoe movies. He had the look down from the disheveled brown suit with trench coat to the scuffed dullness of his patent-leather black shoes. Even his badge looked worn down. He had it pinned to the front of the coat, where it dragged on the cloth like it was trying to take a nosedive off him and escape because it simply couldn't go on.

St. Augustina took the initiative and crossed with her hand outstretched toward the man. "Constable St. Augustina," she said.

The chances of this hardworking detective understanding what the honorifics meant were fairly small, but it was worth a try. He furrowed his eyebrows at her even as he accepted the handshake, giving it a perfunctory double pump.

"Detective Rhodes, Templar Police Force," he said.

St. Augustina's eyes flicked to the TPF acronym on another pin fastened above his badge, which was slowly getting dragged into his badge's escape attempt.

"First on the scene?" she asked, sliding into shop talk easily. "Or was the victim an employee of your corporate sponsor?"

CHAPTER 1

"Corporate sponsor, so we have primary jurisdiction," Detective Rhodes said with defensive edginess. She could practically hear his brain trying to work out who she was and whether she was above him or below him in authority.

She continued her scans around the room, taking in the other techs. "This is Paladin territory," she noted, a fact she had been able to verify after she had gotten the call from her superior about the crime.

"Yeah, well, if they really want to fight me for it, we can take it out to the back alley," Detective Rhodes said dryly just as a uniformed officer came up to hand a two-page report to him.

"Confirmed, sir," the office said. "The perpetrator was a vampire."

"But the cuts?"

"Actually, preliminary says there is the presence of cuts *and* bites, sir, with lots of tearing. Like he was opening her up before drinking—"

"Alright, alright. I get the picture. Dammit," Detective Rhodes muttered as he skimmed the first page. "And he was a resident?"

"Yes, sir, live-in boyfriend."

"Stupid," the detective muttered as he flipped to the second page. "Do we have a name?"

"Officer Boyd is the prime suspect. I'm not even sure who else we could possibly suspect at this point."

"Oh, are you closing my case for me now?" Detective Rhodes asked, dryly, while he flipped to the next page in the report.

"No, sir, I'm just saying, this is an easy one. It's all pretty obvious what happened here. And he was a guard with the Magic Guild," the officer reported as if it were a joke.

To be fair, it was, but the detective didn't seem to think it was funny, giving the officer a long eye of reproach that shut his subordinate up before he had really begun.

"A woman's dead," Detective Rhodes muttered. "Let's cut back the gallows humor."

3

St. Augustina scanned her eyes over the upside-down form while the detective was distracted and letting it hang out in front of him. She winked her right eye, initiating the command for her memory banks to mark the recording for closer inspection later. Then she came to his side to glance over his shoulder as he flipped back to the first page. Her move not only caught his attention but also gave her a clearer look at the front page as well. Right wink, while she thought the word *click*.

"Excuse me," he retorted, then pointedly handed the clipboard back to the officer. Dismissing him with a wave, Detective Rhodes' gaze stayed on St. Augustina. "What jurisdiction did you say you had again, detective?" Then a double-downed look of wariness passed over his face. "Ah, crap, are you telling me you *are* Paladin Policing?"

"No, I'm not."

"Oh, good," Detective Rhodes said, more than a little relieved, "I'd hate to fight a woman today."

"Especially since you'd lose horribly," she countered.

The Detective wasn't done yet. "But you do look like you think you're here to take over my case. You FBI or something?"

"Not anymore, though I've worked for the Bureau," St. Augustina reported truthfully.

Detective Rhodes screwed up his face in consternation and folded his arms. "Well, then who the hell are you and what are you doing here?"

"For a detective, you don't seem to really like mysteries," St. Augustina countered, but her tease didn't seem to do much.

"I don't like being screwed with, lady," he replied sharply.

Internally, St. Augustina sighed to herself. *Ah well, seems like foreplay is over.*

St. Augustina settled back on her heels, slipping her ungloved hands into her pockets to retrieve her prepared business card. She held out the little rectangle with its official Magic Guild stamp to the left of her name, which filled it from one edge to the other.

The detective eyed it but did not take it.

St. Augustina continued to smile. "Constable, not lady. I'm the constabulary representative for the Magic Guild, of which your suspect in this case is a member. I am here to take him into custody per accordance with the Police Treaty of 1918, which grants me the unilateral authority to take any person or persons under the Magic Guild's auspices into custody for crimes committed anywhere in the city of Chicago."

That pronouncement stunned the whole room into silence. Detective Rhodes fish-mouthed for a moment, blinking periodically while his brain metaphorically rebooted before he noticed the room doing the same.

"We don't have all day here people," he called out, and everyone spurred back to the grisly task at hand. "Can I get somebody to throw this woman off my crime scene, while we're at it?" He gave St. Augustina a disparaging look.

"Excuse me, but I am not going anywhere," St. Augustina countered.

"This is a police matter, ma'am. I need you to clear *my* scene, or I will have you arrested for trespassing."

St. Augustina resisted the urge to smirk. *I'd really like to see you try,* she thought. Instead, she said, "Subsection 2A states I have the full authorization to remand Mr. Boyd to my custody."

"Will someone get her out of here?" Detective Rhodes shouted, unimpressed as he turned to walk farther into the apartment.

"Please, if you'll come this way with me, ma'am," the uniformed officer tried to say with honestly more politeness than St. Augustina expected, even as he gripped her upper arm to encourage her along.

To his shock, St. Augustina didn't move a muscle. Her feet didn't even shift as he attempted again with a bit more force.

"Pause playback," St. Augustina said, and the scene around her froze. It was almost comical as she studied each of their trapped faces, held in various unflattering moments. Instead, she turned back to the only other person in the room, the

actual room, who was alive and unfrozen. "As you can see it did not go well."

Through the wall of the apartment, a shadow emerged and formed into the shape of a woman. "I *can* see that," she said. "This technology is amazing."

St. Augustina gestured with her glowing hand, and the world around her became more transparent. The fading of the digital representation of the scene from her perception allowed more features of the woman to appear to her avatar, which floated like a ghost beside her actual body.

The woman's skin was dark and her clothing bright, moving as if to music only she could hear. Lady Ursula, St. Augustina's boss and patron, stood looking about the digital wonder with a pair of black goggles trying to swallow her face. It was the only way for the magical lady to see into St. Augustina's world as the Saint herself saw it. It was a demonstration of the necessity for the jack-in set-up she had purchased with the majority of her new department's budget.

Taking a deep breath that she felt in her actual body distantly, St. Augustina gestured in the air to pull up a menu and initiated jacking-out. A rush of deeper feelings washed over her as her consciousness returned and re-engaged the nerves and fibers of her real body. Like diving out of a pool of water, only in reverse. After the sparky sensations of hot, cold, pain, and pleasure passed, a bell sounded, and she opened her actual eyes.

She sat back in a lounge chair she had scrounged from a gamer's resell shop. She had fitted it with the equipment that allowed her to plug into the port in her neck and become one with the computer interface. Not needing a lot of room for it, she had placed the chair in a spare space attached to the Guard offices in the Magic Guild building, a room someone had decided previously was best used for storage. Various boxes and odd equipment had been stowed above and below what she imagined had been an interrogation table now shoved against one wall. The layout made for some close quarters,

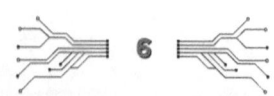

but the interior room had been set up with wards to prevent magic from happening inside, so it minimized interference with her equipment.

"This is different than using a scrying crystal or even the powers of an Oracle Talent," Lady Ursula marveled. She sat upon a pilfered desk chair acquired from the main room. Perched primly upon it, Lady Ursula looked at St. Augustina through the goggles, the dark glass having switched to transparent now that they weren't activated. "It's all so clear ... and real-seeming."

"The tech in my brain acts as a recorder, documenting everything my input interfaces see, hear, touch, and smell. Then with this rig, we can view the memories and interact with them as needed. I can zero in on details and examine a crime scene without having to be at the actual site."

"So, it does not work unless you are within the machine? You are the catalyst?"

"Yes, that is true." St. Augustina nodded as she reinitiated herself back into the digital world and back into the crime scene. The rushing feeling of falling into water then away from her body made her feel queasy for a moment, then she was back, her avatar remanifesting in the digital space.

She gestured again to reset the room once more to the beginning of the memory, restarting her encounter with the crime scene. "This is also admissible in court, so this will be a very useful tool for the cases we choose to take on." She began to shut down the memory, dismissing the translucent walls and figures to leave only her digital avatar standing in the middle of the empty room.

Lady Ursula cocked her head to the side, looking directly at the digital avatar, her body simply a shadow in place of an actual avatar since the glasses weren't set up to produce a specific one in St. Augustina's world. "Cases you choose to take on? But not this case?"

The pause hiccupped between them. "No, this case would not be a good one to start with."

"Why is that?"

"Well, he's clearly guilty," St. Augustina explained. "Templar Police Force took him into custody shortly after and flat out ignored my claims of jurisdiction. So I went over this crime scene earlier, and I would feel very comfortable taking this to a prosecutor. It would just be a matter of waiting for labs to come back with his DNA in her wounds. I would even put some pressure on him to see if a confession is possible; then that's that. Case closed."

"I am not arguing with his guilt," Lady Ursula said with a hint of the stereotypical crypticness so many in the magical community were known for, despite how annoying it was.

"You hired me to help you defend the Magic Guild's people against the corporate policing forces, but even with what you've given me, right now, it is just *me* against a mountain of *them*. If we want this to succeed, I need to be selective about which cases I pursue, at least to start. Trust me, this is not a case you should want me to go to bat on."

Lady Ursula held her silence as she regarded St. Augustina through the goggles. The expressionlessness on the stand-in avatar still seemed to convey her expression of patient serenity.

St. Augustina had a metaphorical premonition that she was going to lose a lot of arguments with her patroness this way. "Here, let me show you what I'm talking about."

The Saint gestured again and brought up another scene from the day before. Instantly, the room expanded and lightened, then filled in with another space entirely, complete with vaulted ceilings that doubled the height of a normal room. Light-colored wood boards covered the floor and stucco-white plastered the walls as she let herself be shifted to the hallway just outside the room; the start of the memory.

CHAPTER 2

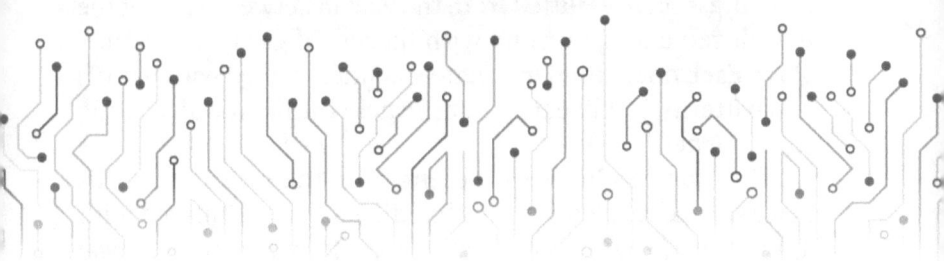

St. Augustina took a deep breath in. Setting her hand on the nondescript, standard office handle, she closed her eyes and focused on her goal. Time seemed to slow around her as she drew the breath inwards to her core.

Her box of supplies stuck into her hip where she braced it with her other hand. She definitely regretted skipping breakfast, since now, her stomach gurgled acid from the lack of something to digest. Otherwise, it felt strange and familiar at the same time to be standing in chunky kitten heels, dress slacks, and a silky dark gray blouse under a long wool coat that went to her mid-thigh. Her false Saint Box rested in full view against the shirt, a black rune-carved thing that hung heavily around her neck, but she couldn't bear to take it off, and she had no intention of hiding it either.

Empty of other people, the hallway she stood in echoed the swishing sound of her breath ever so slightly. Most people wouldn't be able to hear it, but St. Augustina hadn't been like most people for a very long time. She could barely remember

what it was like before her augmentations. She cast her enhanced eye over the hall one more time, memorizing it into her meat brain as much as her mechanical one.

Made of stone, it was truly the strangest hallway she had ever walked down, like something out of a historical movie. All gray stone with tapestries of ancient magic hanging every few feet, complete with elegant small trees at each end in ornately painted pots. The floors were made of marble and covered with sumptuous, well-maintained carpets of red and gold. Brass sconces jutted from the wall in between each of the half-dozen doors, burning with flickers of gas inside cloudy glass. Each door stood in ornate splendor, carved with whorls and patterns, just like the door she held the handle of, waiting to be opened.

But this handle was different from the rest. For all this place's ancient splendor, this handle had been replaced with a dull silver, round knob that one could purchase at a local hardware store. It was hard not to see the metaphor in that as the equally mechanical woman prepared to take over a traditionally magical role.

She took a deep breath.

Turning the handle, she pushed her way through the door into a room filled with talking people.

They all stopped as those inside turned to face their new boss. There were about a dozen of them, dressed in the Magic Guild's designated uniforms: teal polo shirts with the Magic Guild emblem, an eye with an iron cross in the middle, printed over the pocket, and professional black slacks. Some wore caps, but most didn't. St. Augustina noted the stares and their varying degrees of suspicion, contempt, and hostility. She did not respond to it. Entering the room, she turned her own gaze on them and made eye contact with each pair that looked at her, even if only for a second. Eyes were a powerful thing, but these needed to see how powerful *her* gaze really could be.

Some looked away. Some challenged it. Others gave her nothing, so she moved on. Only one had questions written plainly all over her face, full of simple surprise.

Good. She had her start.

St. Augustina came to what she knew would be the door to her office. The rest of the main room was full of wooden desks spread out evenly in the space. A pair of glass windows with nine paneled squares each cast light from the opposite wall. A sub-room in the furthest corner, with its own door hung in some temporary walls that became permanent at some point. It was used as an interrogation room or a holding tank as needed. According to Lady Ursula, they had used it as a storage room lately.

That would need to change.

St. Augustina wanted to take another deep breath in and knew it would be the end of her if she did. It would be like blood in the water to piranhas.

"Good morning," she said, planting herself in front of her door as she tried to sound casual like she was in complete control and expected everyone to comply with that idea. "My name is Constable St. Augustina. I know that can be a mouthful, but to make things simple, just call me Constable."

She gave a professional smile that wasn't returned. They were intent on giving her nothing.

"I'm sure you have a lot of questions, and this is the first day, so I intend to answer them all. To that end, we will be convening in fifteen minutes—"

"It's true," a tall man a lighter shade of brown as St. Augustina interrupted. He folded his thick arms over his chest, his eyes switching over to the opaque white that magic users affected when they were powering up their magic. Even with no other change in the man's physique, St. Augustina knew that this particular Talent, as they were called officially, was a Golem-type. He could turn his skin into a nearly impenetrable armor, which also made his fists weapons on par with baseball bats. She had no doubt that he did it unconsciously. He

was also a vampire. This had been the biggest surprise when she studied the myriad of cultures that came under the Magic Guild flag.

"Is what true, Mr. Boyd?" she asked him.

He didn't react, but those closest to him did, surprised that she knew his name probably.

"That you're a tin man?" he asked, then shifted to lean forward with a sneer. "Tin *woman*."

Well, that was a new one.

"A what?" she asked, arching an eyebrow at him.

"He means, a cybernetically-altered person," a timid coatl, Officer Papaqui, answered. Her serpentine tongue flicked out of her mouth nervously, even as she fiddled with the feathers cresting from her scaly head.

Again, St. Augustina resisted the urge to sigh. Instead, she closed her eyes, counted to three, then triple-blinked them.

The room gasped.

She knew what they saw. One eye glowed blue and the other glowed a bright yellow, blocking out the irises like a Talent's power would. Yet her abilities came, not from a natural magical source, but from within the artificial nanotech forced on her too many years ago. She let them all take the sight in. Might as well get it all out now.

After a full minute, she triple-blinked again, letting her real, dark-colored eyes surface through the light.

"I am an augmented human. I have cybernetic enhancements in my eyes, spine, and various joints granting me senses, strength, and speed far surpassing my natural abilities." She had a few other abilities that her augmentations allowed her, but those were need-to-know, and no one in that room did. "Any other questions?"

"Nope," Officer Boyd said before he plucked up a backpack that had been leaning against his ankles to shoulder it. With a final harsh glance, he turned on his heels and walked poignantly out the door. Before the slab of ornate wood hit the

jamb, seven others followed him, the last one turning back at the last moment to spit in her direction. Silence hung in the air.

"Anyone else?" St. Augustina asked the now emptier room.

The room shifted nervously. "Um, excuse me." A slighter young man in thick glasses raised his hand.

"Montgomery," St. Augustina acknowledged.

"If we walk out right now, are we no longer eligible for our pensions?" he asked.

The coatl officer groaned, dropping her serpentine face into her equally serpentine hand.

"Well, it's an important question," he said in his defense.

"Pensions are determined by years of service, so yes, if you quit now, you lose it," St. Augustina answered simply.

Montgomery sat back down.

"Any other questions can wait until the meeting. Thank you." To emphasize that point, she turned and opened the door to her office, retreating within without seeming like she had done exactly that.

The door closed, and in the darkened room, she took the deep breath she longed for.

That didn't go as bad as I thought it would.

"Pause," St. Augustina commanded from her position at the door, freeing her ability to move in the memory. She turned to the shadow that was Lady Ursula. "And that was the last I saw of Mr. Boyd. In about five minutes from now, Officer Papaqui enters to tell me the rest of the office left, including Mr. Montgomery." St. Augustina gestured with two fingers, pulling down a menu again to select one of the files she had created earlier from what she had seen of the other detective's notes.

"I am sorry; they should not have treated you that way," Lady Ursula said somberly.

"It was not an unexpected reaction," St. Augustina stated. She read from her notes. "Mr. Boyd then proceeded to go with the rest of the office to the 'Usual Bar,' where they drank for several hours. He then returned to his residence and proceeded to kill his live-in girlfriend."

"Yes, I do not doubt the facts of the case," Lady Ursula said. "But he is one of us."

St. Augustina furrowed her eyebrows. "But he terminated his employment—"

"He *is* one of us," Lady Ursula repeated firmly. "You will see many things in your time of service, and I believe you will meet them all with strength and wisdom, but we cannot choose the cards fate deals any more than which side of the dice face up when thrown.

"With all due respect, you hired me to succeed."

"I brought you on to help us recapture something we have lost. Justice. Magic bends rules and complicates people's lives; it takes someone with the principles to serve."

"A Saint's role has always been to get results, not hold on to principles," St. Augustina argued.

"Well, are you a Saint or are you the constable? It is your choice, of course."

With that, Lady Ursula removed the goggles. Without another word, her patron left. The Saint let the digital world around her completely dissolve again and jacked out. Opening her actual eyes, she leaned forward in her chair. Propping her elbows on her knees, she rubbed her hands over her face and groaned.

"Two steps forward, one step back," she lowered her hands to stare out across the space, "is still one step forward."

CHAPTER 3

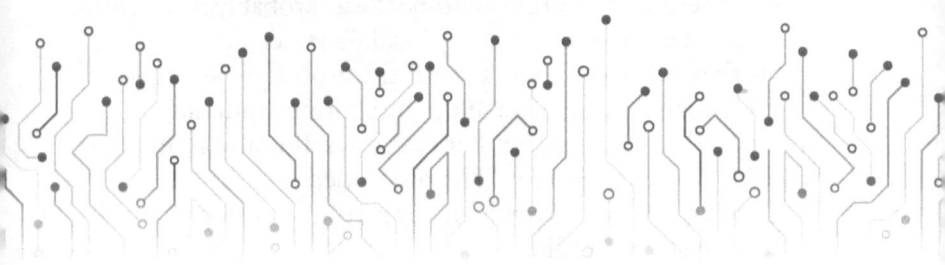

St. Augustina opened the door into the Magic Guild Guard main office.

The large room felt even more abandoned than it did when the occupants originally left with all of their personal effects. She wondered if the guards had all been so fastidious here in MGPD... or was it because they had pre-cleaned out their desks prior to her arrival in preparation for their big "protest demonstration?"

Now there was only one occupant and twenty-five empty desks.

"Crap," St. Augustina muttered to the empty room. Or mostly empty. It did have all the things she had taken out of the storage room. And there was a row of bookshelves behind glass in the back, filled with tomes that made the space seem more like a library than a policing office.

A grinding sound interrupted her study of the room, and she turned to look up in the corner. Sitting on a small shelf in the corner squatted a grotesque, a gargoyle without

the waterspout coming out of its mouth. Everything about it was squat. It had a squat body that sat on haunches with squat claw-like hands and a pair of squat, useless wings. The sneering face stared down at the Saint, but its eyes were blank.

"Okay, that's unnerving," St. Augustina said to it.

The grotesque didn't respond, and after a moment, it shifted its head back up to neutral. Then it stretched, like a chubby cat on its platform, dropped onto its stomach, and stuck its chin on its clawed fist in a perfect image of boredom. Again, it became as still as the stone it was probably made from.

"I am in completely over my head," she decided.

"Is that supposed to be a pun?" the grotesque asked.

St. Augustina gave herself points for not flinching at the thing's sudden speech, but her eyebrows did raise to her hairline. "So, you are sentient," she responded.

The grotesque narrowed its eyes to slits at her. "I am the security system," it said.

"Excuse me, ma'am?" a small voice interrupted from the door just below the grotesque's shelf.

St. Augustina dropped her gaze to see Officer Papaqui standing at the door. The coatl woman stood dressed much as she had been in St. Augustina's recorded memory, in the teal polo shirt with black slacks in addition to the deep winter gear made for people climbing Mt. Everest despite the actual mildness of the winter day. It was maybe thirty degrees Fahrenheit outside at the least. The officer also toted a large satchel over one shoulder.

"Uh, who are you talking to?" the coatl asked.

"Just introducing myself to your grotesque there," St. Augustina said, gesturing up at the statue. It had resumed its previous pose.

"That's ... not a person. It's just an enchanted object. The Magic Guild uses them as a security system without breaking up the aesthetic of the place."

CHAPTER 3

"Did you forget something?" St. Augustina asked civilly, crossing her arms over her chest to lean against one of the abandoned desks.

"Well, you see, ma'am," the coatl said, flicking her tongue out in a clear sign of nervousness while she pushed back the hood of her coat, letting her tri-colored, feathery crest lift free. After a moment, she set her satchel onto one of the empty desks and pulled off the long-to-the-floor coat. "I just couldn't leave, you see. So... I'm here to report for my shift, ma'am." She stiffened up as she said it as if she were preparing to stand at attention and salute, but since it was not a part of the Magic Guild code of conduct, it left the coatl with nowhere to go.

St. Augustina cocked an eyebrow at that statement.

That triggered more tongue flicks. "You see, I have a duty. I swore an oath to protect... I mean, we can't all leave it undefended like this. The Magic Guild, that is. Not if all of us leave. That would be wrong."

"That's very noble of you," St. Augustina said. She had intended to add a "but" to her statement. However, the effect of just saying that much seemed to brighten the officer, warming her scales and fluttering the feathers along her striking crest of red, yellow, and white.

This time, she did actually salute. "Honored to serve," she said.

St. Augustina made a token gesture just to get her one and only officer to be "at ease."

Officer Papaqui relaxed her arm and smiled as brightly as her serpent-like face could smile. "So... um, what are you doing?" She turned to look at the mess that had once been in the storeroom poignantly.

"Just rearranging things. I needed to make some room for some other equipment."

"Do you want some help putting it all back?" Officer Papaqui offered, her cresting raising in place of the eyebrows she didn't have.

"No, actually. Sorting that out is going to have to wait for now. I have ... a case I need to deal with."

"A case?" Officer Papaqui asked, her crest rising again while her blackish red marbles for eyes widened.

St. Augustina's heart grew heavier in her chest. "You haven't heard?" she asked, praying she wasn't going to have to be the one to inform this earnest officer about the crimes committed by her co-worker. It had been the one blessing in all this that St. Augustina wouldn't have had to deal with a shocked and grieving office.

Officer Papaqui stared at St. Augustina, her tongue flicking in and out for a few moments. "Heard what?"

St. Augustina wondered at the wisdom of showing her memory recordings of the crime to the coatl officer. She logicked that if she was going to keep the officer on her employ, she needed to know what sort of "tin woman" she was made of. As the recording ended, with St. Augustina acquiescing to the police that had full possession of the crime scene, her digital-self glanced over at the new shadow sitting where Lady Ursula had been earlier. Getting the goggles on the coatl had been a trick since her face didn't exactly line up with most of the hominal faces it had been designed for. The officer took the oddness in stride as if she dealt with this hang up all the time. St. Augustina made a note to herself to check suppliers to see if there was a serpentine goggles design somewhere online or someone who could make a custom set. She'd buy them if the officer stuck around.

As the recording faded, St. Augustina came back to her actual body in the chair. Opening her real eyes, the interior lights came up to full, illuminating the nearly empty room. Officer Papaqui popped off the goggles to meet her boss' expectant gaze.

"So? What do you think?" St. Augustina asked when Officer Papaqui said nothing.

The officer rested the goggles on her lap as her tongue flicked in and out a moment. Then finally, she said, soberly, "I only met Boyd's girlfriend twice... at the last two office Christmas parties. I've never actually known someone who has died before." She flicked her tongue some more. "My grandmother died before I was born. Degenerative scale disease. It runs in the family. I have to get screenings every year." Her tongue kept flicking.

St. Augustina decided that was a sign of agitation since she had such limited experience with coatls. Everyone processed death differently, even tangential deaths. Maybe especially tangential deaths.

"At those Christmas parties, how did they seem?" St. Augustina asked, resting her hands on her knees.

Flick-flick went her tongue. "Fine, I guess. They seemed like they liked each other." Flick-flick. "Actually, the first time..." The crest rose in a flash of color. "Do you know anything about how coatls... um... you know...?"

St. Augustina cocked an eyebrow. "I'm sorry, I really don't?"

"You know." Officer Papaqui gestured with a hand as if that would help communicate, but the motion meant nothing to the human. "Get it on."

"Oh!" St. Augustina declared, suddenly getting it very clearly. "Uh, no. No, I don't."

This was obviously an uncomfortable subject for the officer, but she stumbled anyway. "Well, you know how ... most snake-based peoples ... when we ... get it on, how we wrap up around each other." That crest couldn't be standing more on end if she had stuck her fingers in a light socket. "They were like that the first year. I... I thought they were doing it right in front of the whole office, but Montgomery explained to me how human-based peoples..."

"How *we* get it on?" St. Augustina supplied when the embarrassed coatl simply couldn't go on.

She pressed her hands against the darkening scales of her face, her version of a blush, shaking her head. "Well, he said for you, it's just foreplay. I'm sorry. I don't see how any of that helps."

St. Augustina burst out laughing. She simply couldn't hold it in anymore. At first, Officer Papaqui startled at the sound.

"I'm sorry, I'm sorry," St. Augustina said as she tried and failed to smother the giggles. "I just—" But it just sent her back into another round.

Papaqui's crest relaxed then, and she too began to chuff what St. Augustina took as her version of a laugh. The tension relaxed in the room.

"No, thank you, Officer. That was very informative," St. Augustina said once the merriment died down; then it went too far in the other direction into heavy soberness.

"Do you think he really did it?" Officer Papaqui asked.

Yes, St. Augustina thought.

"Too early in the investigation to determine," she actually said. "What we have here is a twofold problem. We need to do the investigation, and we need to get jurisdiction back over Officer Boyd, and those two problems are fairly mutually exclusive."

"Former Officer Boyd," Officer Papaqui corrected.

St. Augustina conceded her that. "Indeed."

"And by custody, you mean, they arrested him already?"

"Yes, that is what I generally mean by custody."

"Got it. Okay, so where do you want to start, Constable?" she asked, handing over the goggles to her boss as she stood up.

Hearing the title said out loud actually sent a shiver down St. Augustina's spine, which somehow made it all seem more real.

"I need to talk to an expert on Guild Law. A specialty in how it pertains to vampires would be great."

Officer Papaqui flicked her tongue thinking a moment. "I actually know who you could talk to," she said.

CHAPTER 4

t. Augustina eyed the transfer door. She still did not trust it. There were actually three of them, and all three doors looked the same except for the wooden carved signs above. The Saint faced the one labeled "Lincoln Square." She stared down the dark brass knob.

"Is everything alright, ma'am?" Officer Papaqui asked. The coatl waited beside her.

"No, it's fine," St. Augustina said.

"Do... Do you not know how it works?" Officer Papaqui asked timidly. She checked over her shoulder to see if anyone else heard, but there was no one in the hallway other than the two of them. St. Augustina actually found the officer's concern for her constable's reputation the reassuring sign that it was, even if it was unnecessary.

St. Augustina sighed. "It's how I arrived here. It just..." She swallowed, surprised she was finding this hard to admit. "It gives me the heebie-jeebies."

Taking a deep breath, St. Augustina stopped delaying the inevitable and turned the handle of the door. It opened onto a beautiful fountain courtyard known as Lincoln Square. The transfer door was an impossible magical feat that technology still couldn't replicate. The ability to walk through a door in one place and out into another that was several miles away filled her with awe.

Lincoln Square was a beautiful area, with a statue on one end and the fountain on the other end, empty of water for the winter. Despite the cold, wintery air washing over her, the courtyard was filled with people and children. Several of the kids ran past the door just as St. Augustina was about to step through, crunching the snow and squealing as snowballs flew after them. The constable waited a moment longer for them to clear before leading her team of one through.

Sure enough, the augmented woman shivered as she crossed the wash of weirdness that was the invisible wall of magic hanging in the threshold. She got a slight ping alert from her augmentations along with a small lance of pain behind her eyes. It was a reminder that magic and technology didn't always get along in literal as well as metaphorical ways. As St. Augustina turned to watch Officer Papaqui follow her through, she noted the position in the wall. The transfer door stood to the right of the sorbet shop, also closed for the season, in an otherwise blank wall. From this side, the door looked old and in desperate need of repair and fresh paint.

A few exasperated parents and nannies glanced curiously at the Saint as she exited, but St. Augustina only nodded at them as she reached into her coat's inner lining and touched the row of pockets sewn within to hold her equipment. She needed to make sure nothing had been affected by the wash of magic. Then she adjusted her long coat, reset her badge hanging from a chain around her neck, and proceeded toward the main street. Officer Papaqui pulled the door shut firmly behind them, the Magic Guild emblem winking into existence in the cold sun.

While Christmas decorations had long been taken down from the classical streetlamps and around the bottom edge of the empty fountain, evergreen still clung to everything. Mostly composed of shops, Lincoln Square was a slice of middle class surrounded by a neighborhood of otherwise middle-of-the-working-class, full of cheap housing and rental buildings. Several shoppers were walking up and down the street, stopping occasionally to look at the window displays.

"Have you tried Selamarie's yet?" Officer Papaqui asked, coming up beside the Saint. The coatl's voice came out muffled from under the facemask, goggles, and scarf that hid every inch of her reptilian skin and made her eerie eyes even bigger. "It's a cafe and bakery. They make the best flourless chocolate cake in the city."

St. Augustina peered through the windows, her augmentations assisting so that she could see within clearly. The case of pastries did indeed look delectable, and the menu on the back wall offered freshly made quiche, salads, and two different gourmet sandwiches, changed daily.

"Do you want to try it now?" the Saint offered, realizing she was in fact quite hungry.

"But our meeting...?"

"What time did you say we were coming?" St. Augustina asked, even though she knew very well. Officer Papaqui had done as she said and called someone she knew who could help St. Augustina with her inquiries. Someone who was an expert in Vampire case law. The meeting the officer had set up with them was in thirty minutes, which Officer Papaqui repeated again as pulled back her sleeve to look at her old-fashioned wristwatch.

"Plenty of time. This won't take too long," St. Augustina assured. "We have to eat."

A bell tinkled as the glass door with the stylized name of the bakery opened inward, wafting delicious smells of baked goods over them. A few customers were waiting in line at the cashier near the front, lined up along the glass case. In the

back of the room, a young woman stood behind a podium sporting a sign that said, "Please Wait to be Seated." She and her podium were positioned in front of the next room past some drawn-back curtains framing the entryway. Beyond were tables and chairs, crammed together and over two-thirds filled with patrons enjoying lunch and conversation.

"Can I help you?" one of the bakers, a troll wearing a chef's cap, asked from behind the glass case.

"Yes, I would like to see your manager," St. Augustina said, stepping forward before Officer Papaqui could speak first. There were some confused glances amongst the customers and bakers, but St. Augustina simply affixed her pleasant, professional demeanor to her face.

"I'm the day manager," the troll said, coming around the case as she wiped her hands clean on her apron. The tall hat on her head shifted a little, and the Saint realized her horns were probably tucked inside.

St. Augustina extended her hand to be shaken. "Hello, I'm stopping in to introduce myself. Constable St. Augustina."

The troll hesitated less than an inch from taking the Saint's hand. "Constable?"

As if on cue, the customers who were obviously eavesdropping began to chatter amongst themselves.

St. Augustina continued to smile. Still, that was a better reaction than the MGP's entire force. "Yes," she replied. Then she waited.

The troll held back a beat more, then grasped the waiting hand in a single, uncertain shake. "Nice to meet you, Constable," she said warily. "What can I do for you today?"

Okay, the troll didn't offer her name, but St. Augustina decided not to push it.

"Well, not much today. I mostly wanted to come by and meet the pillars of the district under my jurisdiction. You are a Magic Guild business, correct?"

The question was loaded, and the look in the troll's eyes told the Saint she knew it.

"Yes, yes, we are." She glanced over St. Augustina's shoulder to the recognizable officer behind her. "We don't usually get much trouble, but if we do, we call the Cook County Sheriff's office."

St. Augustina knew that, but she nodded. "Well, you can call me now. I'm here to help in any way I can," she said, pulling a freshly printed business card out of her pocket. She offered it to the baker. The Magic Guild emblem was printed on the left side of the card next to the neat type verifying her title and name along with contact information. "You can reach me directly if you need anything."

"Uh, okay. Thank you. I will," the day manager said diplomatically, studying the card for answers to questions she wasn't asking.

It was a start.

"Okay, thank you. Do you mind if I order lunch?" she asked, passing her the OmniSin Lady Ursula gave her, complete with an account for 100,000 credits. Usually, she would upload the information into her hand's augmentation and just scan that, but she hoped offering something more normal and expected would help the people in her district to accept her. She also gestured to Officer Papaqui. "And whatever she'd like. It smells fantastic in here."

"Oh! Really, are you sure? Thank you," Officer Papaqui answered basically in one breath.

St. Augustina nodded. It was a business write-off either way.

"Uh, yes, yes. Just one moment," the day manager said. She scurried back behind the counter and popped up with an order pad. St. Augustina ordered a seven-mushroom prosciutto frittata and a side salad while her coatl companion got the quiche with sun-roasted tomatoes, artichoke, and gruyere. At the last second, she saw the day manager slip two slices of signature flourless chocolate cake into the box as well.

One store won over, a whole street to go.

CHAPTER 5

"Okay, I think I get it. This was community outreach?" Officer Papaqui said, slipping her winter goggles back over her eyes as they exited the bakery through the side exit door so as not to clog up the front. Another large party of lunchers had just piled in.

"I was also hungry," St. Augustina countered, holding her lunch in the thin cardboard take-out box. Officer Papaqui clenched hers between her gloves.

"Ah, it occurs to me that we'll be eating these at our meeting, maybe we should have brought something for your friend as well?" St. Augustina noted.

"No, don't worry about that. Morlock has particular dietary restrictions," she replied as she moved slightly ahead to take the lead as she knew the way to their destination.

"Like what?" the Saint asked as the pair of them tromped down the snow-crusted street.

She didn't get an answer because that was when they came upon the cow. Or at least the statue of a cow. Or rather a

multi-colored statue of a cow that looked like it walked out of a work of art painted by a drunk student of Picasso. The only thing that made it mildly observable with all the loud, screaming colors was it had a blanket of snow on its back and the dirty Santa hat some art enthusiast/critic had adorned on its head. Officer Papaqui turned at the cow and headed up the street about half a block before turning into a storefront.

A creaking sign above it declared the place "Morlock, Attorney-at-law."

A bell chimed as they entered the main room of the storefront. The place looked like it had been created as a temporary office judging by the cheap plaster on the walls and industrial carpet the catalog probably called "avocado." Three desks and a giant safe took up positions against each wall, creating a zigzagging pattern to the office. Office plants in various stages of dying and piles of papers coated everything, save the last desk in the back. That desk seemed to still be functioning as the manufacturer intended. Seated at it was a man in a vest, tie, and dress pants. His dress coat hung over the back of his chair while he leaned forward flipping amongst three piles of papers. A pen stuck out of his mouth. St. Augustina noted the slip of elongated canine, white against the black plastic surface of the cheap pen.

He looked up at the sound of the bell. "Hello? Can I help you?" he asked automatically, speaking around the pen.

Officer Papaqui slipped off the goggles and pulled down her hood, not that it revealed her face enough for recognition with her additional stocking hat and scarf. Still, the lawyer leaned back in his chair and snapped his fingers beside his head.

"Oh, I remember, uh... Um... yes. Officer..." He finally snapped his fingers into a pointed finger, which he directed at her. "Papaqui, am I correct?"

"Yes, you got it," the officer said pleasantly, then gestured to St. Augustina. "This is Constable St. Augustina. We've come to get some advice from an expert."

At her introduction, St. Augustina moved forward to extend her hand, juggling her lunch box into the other, which the lawyer rose to shake perfunctorily. "Uh, yes, Morlock, attorney-at-law."

"Pleasure to meet you," she responded, and he gestured toward a chair set up in front of the active desk.

"Uh, please sit, and thank you for not laughing at the name. It's my grandfather's. Traditional vampire name. Personally, I hate it."

"Then why don't you change it?" Officer Papaqui asked, dragging a second chair over.

"Because my grandmother is still alive, and she would kill me," he said matter-of-factly then lifted an eyebrow. "Constable?" he questioned.

"Yes, I was just hired at the Magic Guild to fill the position," the Saint answered.

He sat back down with a confused eye. "Uh-huh," he said.

St. Augustina settled her take-out box on her lap, while Officer Papaqui proceeded to shed her various layers of winter gear, her take-out box already sitting in the additional chair.

The shedding seemed like it was going to take a while, so St. Augustina decided not to wait. "We are investigating a case involving one of the Magic Guild's former guards. He's implicated in a murder, and he's a vampire—"

"We're going to prove his innocence," Officer Papaqui added.

St. Augustina flinched at the coatl's words since she was already fairly convinced of the vampire's guilt. She looked toward the attorney. "We need to get him back into Magic Guild custody before we can continue any sort of investigation," she said diplomatically.

"And you've come to see me because I am a vampire who happens to be a lawyer," Morlock concluded as he clasped his fingers together on top of his desk.

"I came to see you because I was told you were an expert on Guild Law and had a specialty pertaining to vampires. I did not know you were a vampire," St. Augustina replied, unbuttoning her coat.

"Oh, trust me, I'm not offended. You're correct, I have a specialty pertaining to Vampiric Law." His gaze was already drifting off as if he had gone inward to start flipping through filing cabinets in his mind.

"Do you think you can help me?" St. Augustina asked.

"This is an official request on behalf of the Magic Guild?"

"Yes," St. Augustina replied. Officer Papaqui finally finished disrobing down to her teal polo and a set of snow pants, then sat in her own chair, settling her take-out box on her lap.

"Then I am obligated, as part of my status as a Magic Guild sanctioned business, to offer the office of the Constabulary this consultation gratis, but anything that takes more time, research, filings, and the like are considered billable at my discretion," he stated as he pulled out a clean legal notepad of yellow paper covered in lines.

"I understand," St. Augustina said as if she already knew that.

He nodded, and they got down to business. "So, what sort of case is it again? You said murder?"

St. Augustina opened her palm and rolled the fingers in a magician's flourish to activate the hologram projector within. Above her palm, a yellow ball of light emerged, then broke apart with a gesture of her fingers through the globe.

Immediately, the light reformed over her head into a miniature of a case board. She tapped several documents on this mini board to expand larger, including a profile list of Boyd and several of the pictures she isolated from her memory of the crime scene itself. The pictures blew up, morphing into full color as they grew.

The vampire's eyes widened at the display of technological marvel. Hardly anyone had sophisticated augmentations such as this, especially not within the magic community. The process of acquiring such tech was incredibly painful and extremely dangerous as the electrical fibers needed to be grafted into living nerves without antiseptic. That meant the

rich and powerful who could afford them were not inclined to do so at least on themselves. The magical community had no such equivalent, so the lawyer's reaction was not surprising, and if she was honest, she *was* trying to impress him.

Then his eyes focused on the crime scene photos and grew even wider. "Is... Is that blood?" Morlock asked, surprisingly alarmed as he pointed at the image.

Before St. Augustina could confirm it, a strange burp erupted from the vampire.

"Oh God!" was all he got out before he scrambled for a metal trash can under his desk and proceeded to vomit violently into it.

Alarmed, St. Augustina jumped to her feet and leaned helplessly on the other side of the desk.

"Oh God, put it away, shut it down!" he pleaded, waving his hands at the images just before another wave of vomit blew out of him.

St. Augustina crushed her hand into a fist, collapsing the images and light into nothing. As she did so, Officer Papaqui tried to go around the desk to help the distressed vampire, only to get blown past as he bolted with his wastebasket in his arms around the wall behind him and into a small bathroom. He slammed the door so hard that the whole temporary wall shook, making the row of his dusty diplomas swing in sync.

The officer and the constable exchanged a look as more sounds of retching continued muffled behind the door.

"What happened?" St. Augustina asked, truly dumbstruck.

Officer Papaqui's eye ridges quirked together as her tongue flicked out with worry. "It's my fault, I should have warned you. I didn't think..." She glanced at the door, then leaned forward a token amount toward St. Augustina. "He's a hemophiliac," she stage-whispered.

Abruptly, the door opened with the snap of a light switch taking away the light. The vampire re-emerged, wiping his mouth with a fairly new-looking hand towel, his hair lightly wetted as if he had splashed cold water onto his face.

"Hemophobic," he barked out as he stumbled back to his desk chair. Once safely in the bucketed thing, he opened a drawer next to him and pulled out a brown bottle and a low-ball glass in a movie-level cliché action. After splashing an unspecified amount into the glass, he imbibed it, then swished it around in chipmunk-rounded cheeks before swallowing. A second round later, and he opened his eyes, breathing like a drowned man who had finally come up for air.

"Are you alright?" St. Augustina ventured.

"Nope," he said with a dry sarcasm that she could appreciate. He poured himself a third drink, but this one, he sipped slowly. "The alcohol helps. Burns out the smell, taste, and memories. And before you ask, yes, 1 am very aware how strange it is that 1 am a vampire and a hemophobic."

"I confess that 1 don't know very much about vampires at all," St. Augustina admitted.

"Well, that is why you're here, isn't it, Constable? To learn what you don't know." The lawyer gestured again to the chair. "Please, go ahead and have a seat while 1 get my heartbeat under control."

"Heartbeat?" St. Augustina said, jarred and unable to check her reaction. This had just been too strange of an afternoon.

The vampire shot her an annoyed glance. "Yes, heartbeat. 1 am a living creature contrary to popular belief." He sighed exasperatedly. "What you're thinking of is a false vampire."

"A *false* vampire?" St. Augustina crooked an eyebrow.

"A dead vampire," Officer Papaqui chimed in. "We call them 'meat puppets' in the office."

"I don't know what you know about magic," Morlock began, "but there are several sorts of magics that can make a body move and act like it's alive. They're all illegal, but that doesn't mean they don't exist. The most common look like us, but they're just demons inhabiting bodies, which they warp with the stolen magic." There was so much bitterness in the lawyer's tone that she could hear the years of resentment of being compared to such creatures. It was the sort of resentment

passed through the generations of a culture. She also knew a thing or two about secret pain.

Just then a series of musical pings grabbed everyone's attention, and Papaqui jumped to dig out a mobile phone from her winter coat. Glancing down at it, she moved to shut it off, then checked herself as she stared at the number unsure of what to do.

"Sorry, ma'am, it's Jodi from the office. I mean ... the former office... I mean... she worked in the office before she quit... I..." She cleared her throat. "She... She must have heard about Boyd. I... I shouldn't answer it, right?"

St. Augustina gestured at the phone. "Go ahead, you might as well. Don't reveal anything about the investigation at this time, but to be honest, I'd like to discuss this matter with Mr. Morlock one-on-one."

"I have a soundproof room for such calls behind that door there to your left." Morlock gestured. "You can go in there."

The coatl acknowledged and scurried in, leaving only a tiny bit of loose feather fluff in her wake. Once they were truly alone, the vampire turned back to the modified human and appraised her levelly.

CHAPTER 6

was led to believe when Lady Ursula hired a Saint that you would be better informed on the people you served than you seem to be," he said, his voice a courtroom neutral.

St. Augustina's heart did a double skip. Luckily, she was trained to not let such bodily inflections show on her face. *Huh, he already knew about constables. Yet, he had seemed so surprised when he met me and heard that there was a constable,* she thought. She reminded herself about the need to check her own biases; she had been assuming everyone in the magical community would be surprised to learn of her. "You know about me," she stated.

Morlock didn't let anything slip on his face either. Instead, he leaned back in his bucket chair and interlaced his fingers over his chest as his eyes studied hers. "I have had dealings with one of *your* kind before, as well as the organization that made you. I know enough to know that what I know is barely scratching the surface."

She felt her whole body still into a deadly tension. He seemed to take the warning for what it was because he restraightened and braced his feet which signaled flight or fight to her. She was prepared for either.

"And what have you scratched up?" she asked, her voice professionally pleasant which had a way of sounding more threatening than a growl ever could.

He set his still clasped fingers onto his desk. "I had the opportunity to examine some of the specs of your construction during discovery in a case."

"*You* did?" she challenged, not believing it.

"Not everything I saw was admissible in court. Not everything I saw came up through ... normal discovery channels. *None* of what I saw was right."

"Why are you telling me this?" she asked, narrowing her eyes.

"Because I want us to be allies, not enemies, and I thought you would find this admission more of a comfort than if you found out in a less opportune time," he said, choosing his words carefully. He probably was the sort that chose all his words carefully. A quality one wants in a lawyer. "I didn't expect to be talking to you so soon, however, or under such unfortunate circumstances."

After a long moment, St. Augustina turned over his careful words, and the tension lessened under her skin. He was right; she needed allies, and those were very thin on the ground.

In turn, the lawyer settled slowly back into his own chair as they came to a silent agreement.

For now.

"There are 77 diverse neighborhoods in Chicago, and all of them have peoples and residents that fall under the Magic Guild's auspices," the Saint stated. He probably knew all this, but it was safer to be clear. "All of them with their own cultures and beliefs, and several of those are divided even further into sub-cultures. That's a lot for anyone to learn."

"But you literally have a CPU in your head," Morlock countered.

"Which is mostly full just running support programs and data sifting for our implants. Memory storage is still connected to my brain, but one that is focused with some different tech allowing me access to those memories in a different way." She arched an eyebrow at the lawyer. "If you really had seen *my* 'specs,' you would know that."

"I'm not claiming I understood everything I read or saw. I'm a lawyer, not an engineer. But if you would like me to recite all of Chicago's laws and by-laws in the municipal code, I would be happy to oblige."

A spark of humor pinged St. Augustina's chest, slipping up to the corner of her mouth to twitch it. "So I think we can both agree we each *know* things, but not necessarily the same things."

"Which is why we need each other," Morlock agreed. "And you would like to know what laws apply to your vampire murder case?"

"Precisely." She moved to reactivate her hologram, but Morlock held up a hand.

"Wait! How about you send me a written report of all the details, and I'll work my way through them at my own pace. It's better for both of us and my plumbing."

St. Augustina had to concede that. "The barebones of what I know is that a couple of days ago, a former Magic Guild Guard allegedly murdered his live-in significant other. There are bite marks, which seem to imply that he drank her blood." Morlock groaned a moment, breathing fiercely through his nose, then nodded for her to continue. "But I don't know what I can use in this case other than the alleged perpetrator's race as grounds to have him moved to Magic Guild's custody."

Morlock sighed, then shifted in his chair to open a drawer. From that, he withdrew a stack of small books bound together with a rubber band. He yanked out one from the middle that was embossed with an eagle and shield on the outside.

"There are two different sets of laws regarding vampires. Living vampires have the same rights as any other living being in the state of Illinois. False vampires, not so much."

"And Boyd is one of the living kind," St. Augustina stated for confirmation.

Morlock nodded. "Yes. In fact, in the interest of full disclosure, his mother and mine are both Lamian." He sighed at St. Augustina's blank face. "Lamians are a vampire clan that heralds from parts of Greece. Several families came over during World War II to escape the mass extinctions. Trust me, they have high expectations for their children. Boyd even more so because his mother married a member of the Obayifo clan, which is a group that heralds from West Africa and that comes with its own baggage."

St. Augustina smiled in recognition. "Believe me, I know a thing or two about parental expectations."

He sniffed at that as if he didn't believe her, but he refocused on the topic at hand. "Regardless, all vampire clans are governed by the same set of laws as everyone else with the exception of what is commonly referred to as Hematophagy Laws, which dictate the rules around... *blood* consumption—"

The lawyer stopped a moment on the word, and for a second, she thought he was going to be sick again. Instead, he closed his eyes, breathing hard through his nose as he grabbed the liquor bottle to down a quick swallow. That seemed to steady him, and after another breath, he opened his eyes and continued on as if he hadn't interrupted himself.

"And the transportation of *you know what* related products for consumption. All monitored by the Magic Guild, and they apply to more peoples than just vampires, but you get the idea."

He flipped through the book, and when he found the page he wanted, he passed it to St. Augustina. She took it, turning it to look at the writing within. It was a miniature version of the laws he just spoke of, and the heading proclaimed the words "Hematophagy Laws" in old-fashioned looking, fancy script.

"That lays out all the things you need to know about what is and is not legal bl—hrm... *you know what* letting," Morlock explained, "but as you can imagine, it is much the same as anything else considered 'intimate contact.' Consent is key and can be very difficult to prove in a court of law. Especially with a ... blood kit." He managed to get the word out followed by a three gulp of liquor chaser.

"I do not know what a blood kit is," St. Augustina admitted while he drank.

"You wouldn't if you've never been bit, but it can be performed at the hospital to determine if there is a presence of vampire saliva enzymes in a person's bloodstream. They can be useful in prosecutions of nonconsensual blood-drinking. Basically, the DNA sequenced can link the vampire to whomever they have bitten within about twenty-four hours. If processed properly." He added the last with a disparagement that left the Saint believing such tests were too often not. "After that, the victim's natural immune defense destroys the enzymes."

"So if Boyd did commit this crime, this enzyme test will prove it," St. Augustina stated her understanding.

"It'll prove he bit his victim within twenty-four hours of her death, yes, but it will not determine if those bites were consensual or not, or if they happened before any other weapon became involved. Those things could be estimated by lividity though. Now with your case, what is likely to happen, is that the prosecution will use the fact that she was bitten at all as compelling evidence because such things do sway juries. It can be hard for juries to understand the nuances when something like a vampire attack happens. There have been cases where a vampire participated in a consensual feeding right before someone else murdered them, only for it to be years before the vampire managed to exonerate themselves, if they manage to at all. Vampire bites associated with a murder are always tested."

They both lapsed into silence while St. Augustina processed all of that.

"Well, this is all interesting, but how does this help me get him back into Magic Guild custody?" St. Augustina asked, staring down the larger problem in the face.

Morlock paused a moment, opened his mouth, thought better of it, then deflated a little. "I suppose it doesn't. If Mr. Boyd was one of these false vampires, he would be considered a thing, instead of a person. That would remand him to your custody for proper disposal."

"I see."

"Did you know Boyd personally?" Morlock asked.

She shook her head. "Not at all. Professionally, I only knew him from his official MGG file and the five minutes he took to walk out in protest of my hiring."

Morlock grunted at that. "Not an enviable first case."

"I don't get to choose the cases, apparently," she countered. "I know what the precedencies are for claiming jurisdiction, but they haven't been enforceable so far."

"Oh, they *are* enforceable," Morlock said, cheering up for the first time in minutes. "There just hasn't been anyone to actually enforce it."

"Really?"

He nodded enthusiastically. "Oh, yes. Historically, the Illinois Supreme Court has upheld the Magic Guild's jurisdiction over crimes involving its members, of which Boyd positively qualifies. Your trick will be to find a Magic Guild-sanctioned judge."

"And you just so happen to know someone I can call upon?" St. Augustina asked hopefully.

He snorted. "There hasn't been an MG-sanctioned judge for a while that I would trust. Most of them aren't even in the community, even if they are non-hominals, but the Inner Council had to designate somebody, so?" he hissed through his teeth as he shrugged. "Welcome to Chicago."

St. Augustina sat to think that over. "I suppose who am I to complain? It can be said they did the same thing with the constable position."

"Indeed, it can," Morlock agreed, though he didn't seem to mean it as a negative, just simply a fact.

"What are the qualifications to get appointed as a judge?" she asked.

That paused the lawyer for a moment. "Well, traditionally, they have chosen someone who has been an already existing court judge. But that is not the exact letter of the law." She could see the wheels turning in his head, his fingers twitching as if he were paging through a book in his head. Probably he was.

"So, someone like you could be appointed as a judge?" St. Augustina said, looking pointedly at the lawyer.

Morlock blinked out of the middle distance and met her eyes with a cocked eyebrow.

"I have no interest in being a Magic Guild judge at this time."

"Oh, I know, I'm just asking. Hypothetically."

"Hypothetically?" he repeated as if he didn't believe her, but he conceded to her thought experiment. "Yes, I think you could appoint any officer of the court to be a Magic Guild judge. Technically, all one needs is to be licensed by the Illinois Bar Association. It's just traditionally—"

"Yes, and traditionally, the Magic Guild had its own fully staffed law enforcement office with a contingent of designated deputy constables running it."

"I suppose so," Morlock conceded. "These have been different times we're living in." He held up a finger. "I know you're doing what you need to do to make this work, but I would caution you about flouting too many traditions. One could say our traditions are the glue that holds the Magic Guild together."

"But are they traditions only because they've been the status quo so long no one can remember how it was to do things better? And if picking at this glue can solve my jurisdiction problem, then needs must." St. Augustina stood up, still holding her lunch and getting hungrier by the moment. "Thank you for the consult. I'll be in touch if I have any more questions. I'm sorry about the..." She gestured to the bathroom

vaguely, hoping that would suffice since she didn't dare use the word that set him off in the first place.

"It's my cross to bear," he acknowledged as he opened his middle front desk drawer and withdrew a gray card from inside to offer to her. "Call me with further questions; that's my direct mobile number. As long as it doesn't require me filing or researching anything, I won't charge you. Call it my contribution to the cause."

St. Augustina took it gratefully. "Thank you."

CHAPTER 7

I nstead of heading straight back to the office, the next two hours were spent essentially repeating the same process as what she did in the bakery. Moving up and down the street of Lincoln Square, she stopped in to introduce herself and pass out her business cards.

Most shops shook her hand, many gave her suspicious looks, and all took her card. Officer Papaqui chatting beside her helped because she seemed to know most of the people in the stores they visited. The Saint didn't mind the assistance of added legitimacy.

It enabled her to use her augmentations to do quick research on each person of the varying races that they met in real-time, including her coatl sidekick.

The coatls are a very social people. Their social cues are often conveyed through tongue and feather signals, so they have a harder time reading other races' expressions, she read from the overlay displayed through her ocular implant. That she had figured out for herself, but it was interesting to watch in action

as well as the various other races' responses to it. Most took her forms of expression in stride as normal.

Still, by the time they reached the last shop on the street, St. Augustina was simply emotionally exhausted. Socializing had just not been something really required of her in her previous life. She gave orders to subordinates and they obeyed. Community outreach was just not a thing.

But she was a constable now.

"You okay, boss?" Officer Papaqui asked, catching her staring off in thought. They had been walking down the street, and thankfully, they were almost at the end.

"After this last shop, I'm going to call it a night. I'm getting hungry," St. Augustina said.

"Oh, yeah. We probably should have eaten at the cafe. I was just planning on heating up my quiche when I got home, but fresh is really good too."

St. Augustina let her continue to ramble as she pulled open the last glass door on what seemed like a knitting shop, judging by the baskets of brightly colored yarns on display.

"Can I help you?" a sweet, mild voice asked.

"St. Augustina," the Saint said offering her hand to the pretty little faun in a multi-colored apron. The faun's hand was slight, like it was boned with twigs, but the callouses on her fingers were tough like the pads of ... well ... a deer.

"Clara," she said softly, her long deer-like ears twitching as they stuck out of an equally multi-colored knitted cap. Other than the dark deer-like nose, her other features seemed very human. The whole combination made the woman unequivocally adorable.

The Saint nodded and offered her card along with her spiel, explaining her presence. The faun listened politely, but before the Saint finished, the faun's ears twitched to straight up, crumpling the cap together.

"Ma'am?" Officer Papaqui asked, picking up on the signs of agitation, her own crest rising.

Then the store's main window filled with flashing blue light.

"Crap, it's Paladin Police," Officer Papaqui muttered.

"Well, that took longer than I thought it would," St. Augustina said glibly. "Anyway, like I was saying, you can contact me any time; we are here for you should you need us."

The faun nodded, but neither her eyes nor her ears turned back to St. Augustina as the door jingled. "Please, I don't want trouble," she whispered, taking a timid step back, bumping into one of her display baskets full of different shades of purple merino wool.

Two officers, in dark winter uniforms, bearing overladen black belts with everything from guns to giant flashlights, swaggered into the store. The set of an old western movie would have groaned.

St. Augustina lifted her hand toward them and gestured to initiate her augmentations eidetic memory storer, capturing an image like a camera, her gesture focusing it on the two figures. In her vision, she isolated the two faces and initiated a search to run in the background. Only Officer Papaqui seemed to notice the gesture, flaring her feathers a second before her attention got pulled back to the two Paladin officers.

"We got a call concerning a disturbance on this street," one of them said, a balding man who clearly carried his feelings in his beer gut.

"There are no disturbances here, Officer Ed," St. Augustina said fairly pleasantly as she turned to face them.

The balding officer's steps skipped a beat as she accurately named him. He looked her up and down with a sneer creeping up his nose. "I would like to ask you a few questions," he stated.

"And I'll be happy to answer them," she returned, as she quickly read what her search had pulled up of his file.

She was grateful that during her short time with the Paladin Police, she had demanded and been granted a full list of the personnel available from which to pull her team from. That information was still stored in her augmented memory, and Officer Ed had been clearly unfit to make any of her lists. The official complaints listed against him were too long to read even for her enhanced abilities. A small part of her hoped that this encounter would end in the need for her to kick his ass. But that was just a small part.

"What's your business here?" he demanded, the sneer coming out of his eyes now.

St. Augustina held out one of her business cards. "I'm just introducing myself to my constituents. I am the new constable of the Magic Guild, St. Augustina."

He stared at the business card as if she had handed him a fecal sample, but he took it, then he thrust it at his partner without looking at it. "Let me see your OmniSin. Now," he barked, pulling a reader off his encumbered belt.

Feeling her MGG officer bristle behind her, St. Augustina smirked. The smirk had the added effect of making Officer Ed narrow his eyes even smaller. It wasn't the reaction he expected.

With a triple blink, her eyes ignited. The second Paladin police officer gasped at the sight, while Ed's own eyes widened into near-perfect circles. Now, he looked unsure, the perfect moment. Opening her palm, St. Augustina initiated a hologram from it, bringing up the digital version of her OmniSin.

"Crap, she's a cyber-something. Ed, she's cyber," the partner said urgently barely managing to pitch his voice down.

"Shut up, I can see..."

St. Augustina ran her hand over Officer Ed's reader before he was ready. It didn't matter. Immediately, the light on the top flipped to blue, the sign of executive privilege. Every Saint had it. Very few truly knew why. Behind her, she felt Officer Papaqui startle. Glancing over her shoulder, the coatl's eyes were wide.

"Blue status," she breathed, again surprising the Saint that she actually did know what that meant. The kind of hardware St. Augustina had, people for-went mega-yachts to pay for what she carried under her skin.

Now Officer Ed shifted on his feet, the first sign that he might be realizing he made a big mistake. "Okay, fine," he

stated, regrouping, "Now, I'm going to have to ask you to leave and this fine young..." he glanced at Clara, who had made her way all the way to the far wall on the other side of the lone counter with a cash register, "...woman's establishment."

Yet, St. Augustina knew if she backed down now, the authority and legitimacy of her office would irreparably be damaged within the magical community. She also wasn't looking for a showdown right then and there. It had been hard to plan for this moment because it depended on what kind of person answered the inevitable call to come out and intimidate her. A quick glance over the officer's shoulders showed she had an audience too. Several people from up and down the street were staring through the front window like they were watching a show on a very large TV.

She was going to have to accept a draw.

Twiddling her fingers beside her leg, St. Augustina initiated the hack into their radios. It took barely two seconds to find their frequency and broadcast her pre-recorded message to them.

Officer Grossman, the younger officer according to his file, grabbed his radio that was connected to his shoulder.

"Ed, we gotta go," he said, his eyes getting wider as he listened to the dispatch calling them to a scene elsewhere. The same message came through Officer Ed's radio as well, his lips thinning to a straight line as he listened without breaking eye contact with her. *Aw, it's cute. He's trying to win a staring contest with me,* she thought, which was stupid since her eyes were completely opaque.

"Fine, let's go," he growled, with enough arrogance to put a cat to shame. He pointed a finger at St. Augustina's nose. "And you, stay out of my way."

Then they both turned and left.

St. Augustina watched, not just the departing officers but the crowd outside on the street, huddling together and buzzing to each other. The officers ignored it, got into the car, and fired up the siren before pulling away.

"They're just going to leave like that?" Officer Papaqui said, disgust evident in her voice. "I mean, if they thought you were a threat, shouldn't they have walked you out first?"

"They do see me as a threat. That's why they ran away," St. Augustina said, keeping her gaze focused outside. Then she turned to the shop's owner, Clara. "Apologies for the disturbance. Have a nice day." And with that, she left the shop herself.

The crowd outside dispersed as they talked about what they had seen amongst each other. It didn't do to dwell now, so St. Augustina led the way back to the transfer door and back to the office.

Well, that was a full day's work, she thought.

CHAPTER 8

By the time they got back to the Magic Guild office building, it was closer to dinner than lunch. She still carried her take-out tray untouched. Now she felt like she could have eaten her own arm off. Being a Saint burned a lot of calories.

"We'll head over to the judicial offices tomorrow," the Saint said as she waited for Papaqui to follow her back through the transfer door. "Are you alright?"

"It's just, I'm a cold-blooded creature, so as you can imagine, we don't do so well in these cold temperatures," Officer Papaqui overexplained as she shook out a little control device from one of her sleeves. "If this internal heater stopped working, I wouldn't have been able to walk on my own for very far."

"I totally understand," St. Augustina assured, though to be fair, she really didn't. *Why on earth would a cold-blooded person want to live in a place like Chicago? The winters here can be brutal, and it's mild right now,* she thought, not for the first time.

Turning, she led the way to their office.

"All things considered, I think we should both just call it a day," the constable said as she reached for the door handle.

"But ... there won't be anyone on duty in case of a call during the night?"

"There wasn't going to be anyway. You all walked out, and while I can stay up for hours longer than most people, I can't do it in perpetuity. It'll take some time to get a full staff," she countered as she pushed her way inside. "Some services will just be on hold for the time being until I can start taking applications for staff."

"Ah, that explains why there is no receptionist here to greet me," a familiar voice called out, making St. Augustina jump nearly out of her skin.

"Mom!" she cried, stopping so fast that Officer Papaqui banged into her back and dropped her own lunch take-out.

"Aw," Officer Papaqui bemoaned as she bent to pick it up while St. Augustina's eyes bugged out of her head as wide as her mouth.

"What are you doing here?" she asked.

"Well, I came to see your new office," her mother said as she turned to gesture to the empty, unkempt space.

The Saint wished she could sink into the floor. "I ... well ... Mom, I..."

"This is your mom?" Officer Papaqui stepped around, and then quickly bobbed her head, which meant bobbing her whole body since she was still overly swathed in winter gear. "It is a pleasure to meet you Ms. St. Augustina."

"Oh, no, her name is not..." St. Augustina tried to correct, but her mother had already taken charge, extending a hand to her officer.

"Simone Robinson," she said.

"Oh... uh... Officer Papaqui," the coatl person replied, taking St. Augustina's mother's hand in return.

"So you work in this office?" Simone asked, not letting things slip into more awkward silences.

"Yes. Yes, ma'am," the officer said, straightening up, "I just couldn't leave my post with everyone else."

A groan escaped St. Augustina's throat, making both of them look at her.

"Well, it was a pleasure to meet you," Simone said, allowing her officer to disengage gracefully.

"And you ... ma'am," Officer Papaqui returned.

"I'll see you tomorrow," St. Augustina said, giving her officer a none-too-subtle push toward the door.

"Right. See you tomorrow, Constable."

St. Augustina wished she could feel relief once her officer had left, but she had been the one left behind ... with her mother.

"I wish you hadn't come just yet," St. Augustina said.

"Idrina, you didn't have to send her away," her mother scolded gently.

"Yes, I did. I have nothing more for her to do today." St. Augustina pushed her way past her mother to head toward her office, still carrying the take-out box that she really needed to eat. Almost predictably, her mother stopped her in her tracks by grabbing her free hand.

Shorter than St. Augustina by a head, her mother's grip was still as strong as she remembered. While her body didn't have the overall strength it had when she had served in the army, Sgt. Simone Robinson's thickened appearance and gray hair hid what had always been true about her mother. She could kick anyone's ass if pushed.

"You look tired," her mother said, reaching up to brush back a section of curls falling into her face.

"I am tired, Mom. Things haven't started out so great," St. Augustina said, turning and succeeding this time to make it to her office. She held the door so her mother could follow her in.

"You said this wasn't going to be easy when you took the job," her mother stated as if St. Augustina didn't already know that.

"I haven't had lunch yet, you don't mind if I eat?" St. Augustina asked as she rounded her desk to sit down.

"It's getting to be pretty late?"

"Yes, Mom. I'm aware."

"So, what happened? Did they all walk out on you on the first day?"

"In a nutshell." She dropped into her chair and put her head into her hands, awaiting her mother's know everything judgment to fall on her—except her mother didn't say anything.

Oh great, it's worse. She's so ashamed of my failure that she can't even speak to me, St. Augustina thought, daring to look up.

Her mother looked ... concerned. "You know, child, maybe—"

"I already know what I'm going to do! Okay?" St. Augustina sat up sharply in her seat. "I've already got a plan. I can handle this. I don't need advice, and I don't need suggestions. I know you feel guilty or like you got to parent me or something because we lost so much time, but I'm not a kid anymore, and I've been training my whole adult life to deal with this, and I got it, okay?"

She regretted every word as it fell out of her. She even shook her head as she said it.

"I just wished you had told me you were coming; I wasn't ready, and I've got this case already that I'm in the middle of solving, and this is a really bad time for you to just show up and throw wrenches in everything. I know this was going to be hard and that I was probably going to get rejected anyway, but it is part of the plan, okay? I just don't need any comments from you right now, because I got to figure this out on my own or it isn't going to count for anything!"

"Idrina! Stop yelling at me!"

"Yelling? I'm not yelling!" she yelled.

"Child take a breath! I was just going to ask you if I could take you to dinner!" Her mother looked around. "Do you have one of those little office fridges or something you can stow that in? Maybe for your lunch tomorrow?"

A sob escaped St. Augustina's mouth, like a violent hiccup. Her mother stared at her, and that just made it worse. She covered her face, unable to stop now that the floodgates were open. Her mother bent her over in half to pull her into a hug, but she didn't care. She wanted to be small enough again to climb into her mother's arms.

"It's not like I didn't know they were going to walk out. I was prepared for it! So why am I crying?"

"Just because you see the punch coming, child, doesn't mean it doesn't still hurt," her mother said, patting her back, then urging backward. "Here sit down, my girl, oof! I don't remember you being so tall!"

She complied, letting her weight drop into her office chair, which did put her back at the right height to hug her mom easily.

"I... I don't ever cry this much... this is weird," she argued.

Her mother rubbed her arm. "Yeah, that is my fault too. Mothers have a way of bringing out the inner child in us all."

Taking a shuddering breath in, St. Augustina sat back, getting ahold of herself again. "I can't let this happen. I can't let myself fall apart like this."

"You just fell apart in front of your mother, and who am I going to tell? Now, do you want that dinner?"

She nodded. "Yes, please. Ma'am."

That brought smiles to both their faces. Then her mother cupped her chin to look at her. "Ah, my Idrina. I know you will face any and all challenges ahead of you, and you will find your place in all this."

St. Augustina wiped her face quickly. "Not very likely. I got handed this case." She stood up and went to a cabinet in the office, pulling open one of the enchanted drawers there. A burst of cold wafted over her face as she tucked the lunch inside and shut it. "I can't really discuss it but the problem is, it's morally gray and ... I mean I'm not an idiot, I knew there were going to be tough calls like this, but right out of the gate, they want me to advocate for someone who is clearly guilty."

"And they want you to not seek justice?" her mother asked, her tone hardening at that idea.

She slid the cold drawer closed. "No, not exactly. They want me to move him back under their jurisdiction to try. I get it, the greater political implications, but already there is pressure from the community at large to 'save' him from the system. But he's guilty. I mean, *if* he's guilty..."

"So, you have already pre-judged him?"

"What? No, that's not..." she huffed. "I'm not really supposed to discuss the case with you ... and that's not what I'm struggling with." She pushed her hands into her suit coats pockets, fiddling with the things inside them. "I'm just tired of ... gray. You know. I thought this whole thing would be more ... honorable and I could finally leave." She huffed again, shaking her head. "It was stupid of me to think that. To think that anything would actually change."

"Oh, child," her mother said, shaking her head. She even had the nerve to put her fists on her hips as she did it.

"That's easy for you to judge," St. Augustina snapped, turning back to sit behind her desk.

"Child, when I served in Iraq—"

"You won a purple heart for honorable service!" she finished for her, having heard it all so many times during her teenagehood.

Automatically, her mother's hand went to her side, where the shrapnel had penetrated. Some of it still lingered, a greater badge of her honor and courage than one the government could bestow on her.

But she didn't want to fight, or even argue with her long-lost parent. "This isn't what I want. I'm sorry," she stated. The tone undercut the apology, but it was the best she could do under the circumstances.

Her mother raised her hands in surrender. "I just want to say one thing, without interruptions, and then we can drop it."

A third huff. "Fine," she replied.

"When I served in Iraq," she hesitated as she waited for another interruption, but this time St. Augustina held her tongue by griping her armrests, "there were a lot of things I was asked to do that were gray on a good day. Honor is not found in your deeds. It's what you bring to each and every situation."

St. Augustina snorted. "It's a little late for me, *mother*," she growled.

Her mother sighed and shook her head. "If I take you to dinner, can we both agree to not talk anymore about any of this tonight?"

Numbly, she nodded to that.

"Good, because I have more pictures of the grandbaby, and if I don't show them to someone soon, the world is going to end. Now come on. You can pick whichever place you like. You got all the choices in the world."

CHAPTER 9

St. Augustina stood waiting with her hands behind her back as the judge continued to read. He was everything she pictured a judge to be. Older, portly, with silver to white hair cut neatly close to his skull, he wore bifocals perched near the tip of his nose that threatened to fall off at any moment. Behind him on a coat rack hung his black judge's robe, and before him on the desk was a gold embossed gavel resting on a stand with his name engraved below: *Judge Alonzo Alvarez-Hughes*. Beside him, on a wall bookshelf, was a line of propped-up degrees and awards, including one with the same insignia as on St. Augustina's badge, the only sign in the entire room that this man had any affiliation with the Magic Guild at all.

Beside St. Augustina, Officer Papaqui held still, or at least, as still as she could. Her crest kept gently pulsing, giving away her anxiety in a way that her alien eyes simply could not. She held her coat folded over her arms, but since they hadn't been invited to sit, neither divested their winter attire more. After

the day they had trying to get someone to meet with them, this was the furthest they managed to get with any of the "magical-sanctioned" judges. His lack of courtesy be damned if this worked.

At last, Judge Alvarez-Hughes leaned back and slipped off his glasses. He still stared at the papers as he squeaked back in his chair. Clearly, his brain was still within the pages.

"You don't have enough of a case," he stated plainly.

"Excuse me, sir?" St. Augustina said, not expecting that answer at all.

The judge looked up at her, a flicker of apology in his eyes, then he straightened. He slipped the glasses off and folded them into a small container. "Or rather, you have a case, but it's not strong enough to go to bat for."

St. Augustina narrowed her eyebrows. "Excuse me, sir?" she said this time with a hint of menace in it.

He froze as he slipped the glasses case into his front shirt pocket, looking up at her with cold gray eyes. "Don't take that tone with me," the judge admonished. "I am telling you the truth as it is, instead of avoiding you like my colleagues are doing, so I would appreciate the courtesy."

Well, that answered *that* about getting a second opinion.

He stood up from the desk and revealed his dress coat hanging behind him on his chair. He removed it and slipped it on as he spoke. "Now on the legal merits, technically, yes, Mr. Boyd here should be remanded to your custody. In practice, though, there is nothing in this case outside of Mr. Boyd *being* a vampire that warrants the special consideration that only the Magic Guild can provide."

"But sir..." Officer Papaqui protested, but he held up a hand to stop her while St. Augustina reached out for her file still sitting on his desk.

"Based on what you have here, and I won't ask you how you got this much, what you have here is a straightforward murder case that anyone with half a brain can solve," he said simply.

"Any of my fellows would tell you the same. This was a crap case to pick for your first as the new Magic Guild Constable."

St. Augustina ignored the chiding, condescending tone. "So, if I could bring you more evidence of a magically-influenced crime, you would sanction the transfer?"

The judge paused as he reached for his winter coat hanging opposite his judge's robe. He sighed as he let his hand rest upon it. "I suppose this is what I get for talking to you," he said.

"Sorry, sir, is that a 'yes'?" Officer Papaqui said with a squeaky hope.

"It is my duty, and frankly the duty of any Magic Guild-sanctioned city judges, to review all requests from the constable," he said. "Now, if you will excuse me, I am already late to meet my wife for dinner." He testily yanked on his winter coat and held out his hand toward his door in a clear indication for them to go.

St. Augustina met Officer Papaqui's eyes and nodded toward the door. The officer pursed her lips together, held back something more she wanted to say, and obeyed her superior by heading for the door. For the Saint's part, she turned back to the judge and stopped him with her outstretched hand to shake.

"Thank you for doing me the *courtesy* of meeting with me, Judge Alvarez-Hughes."

To his credit, he didn't hesitate to take her hand, shaking it properly. "I was not sure what to think when we were informed that someone from the corporate world had been given the role of the Constable of the Magic Guild. I had hoped this was not a bad sign for the direction things are continuing to go."

"I don't plan on disappointing," St. Augustina said smoothly.

"Hmm, a little late for that," he muttered, but she heard it as clearly as if he had said it boldly.

She felt her muscles knot in her jaw and back of her neck. Covering her anger before it got away from her, she escaped this unpleasant meeting by following Officer Papaqui out the door. The judge shut it firmly behind them and didn't emerge again until their elevator dinged. He probably was waiting for them to leave before he made his own escape, his waiting wife be damned, just to avoid any continuing awkward conversations. St. Augustina could appreciate the sentiment. She had had her fill of Judge Alvarez-Hughes' company too.

"That—" Then Officer Papaqui hissed, clicked, and chirped words that St. Augustina didn't understand but sounded more correct coming out of Papaqui's mouth than her English did.

"You want him to do what to his mother?" St. Augustina asked.

Officer Papaqui turned; her crest fully raised in surprise. "You understood what I said?" she asked alarmed.

The Saint grinned and shook her head. "No, no, but it wasn't hard to guess."

Slamming her winged hat hard enough onto her head to flatten down her crest, Officer Papaqui spat. "I can't believe he spoke to us like that."

"I can," St. Augustina noted as she led the way out of the elevator and toward the street. She paused to sign them out at the desk and barely got an acknowledgement for her trouble. "As unpleasant as he was being, he *did* do us the courtesy of talking to us, which *is* a lot more than his colleagues have done. It at least saves me from having to go to Lady Ursula to force one of them to talk to me."

"Then what are we going to do?" Officer Papaqui asked, muffling her own voice as she wound her scarf around before following St. Augustina out into the winter chill. The sun hadn't set yet, but it would be doing so soon.

"We do what he says. We find more evidence," St. Augustina said. She turned onto the street to head toward the Opener Shop to get a quick way back to the Magic Guild office building. Officer Papaqui scurried up beside St. Augustina. "You know, officer, it's almost the end of the day. If you would rather call it early and head home, that would be fine."

"What are you going to do?" the coatl asked, turning her whole body in order to look at St. Augustina.

"I'll be at the office. I'm going to re-examine the crime scene."

Officer Papaqui nodded her whole body. "If it's all the same to you, ma'am, I would like to come too. The job's not done yet."

A smile quirked at St. Augustina's mouth. "Oh, I could use a dozen more of you," she said softly.

"What?" Officer Papaqui asked, turning herself back toward the Saint.

"I'll get the door," she covered instead, grabbing the handle of said glass and metal door covered with a stencil of an eye hovering within another, smaller door shape. As the Saint held the actual one open, Officer Papaqui tromped in to greet the Opener waiting inside.

St. Augustina tried not to marvel at the room within, which was filled basically with the same door on every wall, crammed within inches of each other and all with the same cheap doorknob.

Officer Papaqui yanked off her glove and fished out her badge from the inner pocket of her coat. "MGG for a direct Opening to the Guild Headquarters," she said.

The attendant, a young woman with a messy bun, askew apron, and very snappy gum glanced at the badge, let out a woosh of fruity air, and got off her stool. Coming around her little counter, she pulled on a ring full of keys and fished out one with a teal end. The whole mess extended on a slim metal wire as she stuck it into the nearest door and opened it. A shiver of wrongness rolled over St. Augustina, and she couldn't avoid the mirroring reaction going up her spine into her shoulders. The young woman cocked an eyebrow at St. Augustina's reaction.

"Well, hurry up, it's not going to last," she said with a bored air.

Officer Papaqui stepped through the watery wall of nothing without hesitation, forcing St. Augustina to do the same. Small spikes of pain thrummed at each of her joints, then abated immediately. As they abated, the pair found themselves standing in the Magic Guild Guard offices, exactly how they had left it that morning, with only Officer Papaqui's desk filled with her things and papers, the rest shoved back against the wall. The only thing that was wrong was that everything around them was black, gray, and white, like they had stepped into a 1950s sitcom. Just as St. Augustina registered that idea, color bled into the space, making the world seem more real. Then it was real.

At last, the door behind them slammed shut, making the Saint jump and spin.

It was just a door.

In fact, the room was simply the room. There were no other signs of the weird magic about the place. St. Augustina glanced up at the grotesque staring down at her. Slowly, its tongue slipped out from between its lips. She had assumed the experience would have been like the transfer door, but that had been ... heebier and jeebier.

"Okay then," St. Augustina said softly.

"What?" Officer Papaqui asked as she divested herself from all of her winter gear. Her crest erupted from under the cap in a flurry of colors as she ruffled the feathers back up.

"Nothing. I just... I'm not used to that yet." St. Augustina slid off her own coat and tossed it along with her gloves onto one of the empty desks before heading toward the back corner where her setup lay. She didn't bother to flip on the light.

Her chair currently sat in an upright position awaiting her. When she was ready to jack in, the chair would assume a more lounged position, which cradled her body. It had been easy to run the wires through the pre-drilled holes on either side of the armrests, one side for her neck port plug-in that went directly into her brain and the other side with the few life-sign monitors she would wear while jacked in. Depressing the switch, the whole thing came to life. The hum under the chair shifted it back into the cradling position, while the bank of monitors above the chair shifted down into position, six in all directed toward her.

"What should I do?" Officer Papaqui asked, peering through the door, her eyes wide. Though if that was from amazement or from the dark, St. Augustina couldn't tell. It was still a new thing in this magical world after all.

"Come in," St. Augustina said, "Grab the goggles and use this." She held out a pair of gloves. "This will allow you to interact with everything in a limited way.

"Wow," Officer Papaqui said, unabashedly amazed as she slipped the gloves on, and immediately, one of her talons pierced through the material. "Oops."

"It's fine, you didn't hurt anything," St. Augustina lied. What she meant was none of the sensors had been ruined, but those were a new pair of gloves. Assured, Officer Papaqui pulled the gloves the rest of the way on, piercing each finger with a talon, then slipped on the goggles.

She turned her head back and forth then lifted them off. "I don't see anything."

"I haven't jacked in yet," St. Augustina said, slipping the finger cuff of the heart monitor and brain monitor onto the index and middle finger of her left hand.

"Jack in?" the officer asked as she leaned forward to look up at the monitors displayed before St. Augustina.

"Yes, it is the term we use when someone transfers their consciousness into the computer set-up. You saw me do it yesterday," St. Augustina explained patiently as she made an adjustment to her seat before she picked up the jack-in plug.

"Oh, of course. Sorry, boss," Officer Papaqui said, her feathered crest pulsing again since it couldn't really convey drooping with the goggle strap holding it down.

St. Augustina lifted up the goggles so she could hold her jack-in plug for her subordinate to see. "When I insert this into this port here on my neck," she gestured the end of the port toward the port in her neck, "I essentially become an extension of the computer, as my consciousness is joined within it."

"Wow!" Officer Papaqui breathed, tentatively touching the jack-in plug as if she expected it to bite her.

"We should have gone over this yesterday, but..." *I hadn't decided I was hiring you yet,* she thought. "But you should know this now that you're working with me," she said. "There is only one circumstance where anyone should pull this cord out of my neck while I'm jacked in," St. Augustina warned, lowering her voice into deadly seriousness. She had the officer's full attention. "If you hear me call for a 'Dorothy,' you pull this thing out of my neck immediately and *only* when you hear me say that word. It will hard jack me out."

"And if you don't jack out properly, it could fry your brain in the process," Officer Papaqui said instead of asking, surprising St. Augustina.

She cocked her head at the coatl. "Did you already know that?" St. Augustina asked.

"I've worked with computers before. My first job was in data entry. Not that your brain is the same thing, but yeah, I imagine it's the same idea. Data loss, brain loss if the cord gets pulled or under sudden power loss the CPU can fry, that kind of thing."

"Well, if we have a power loss, I have a backup generator that will immediately switch over, so I have time to jack out, but yeah, you have the basics." Feeling more assured than she had a few moments before, St. Augustina leaned completely back into the chair. "Okay, you ready for this?"

"Yes, ma'am," the coatl said as she set her fingers on the edge of the frames, preparing to slide them down. She glanced at the screen that showed St. Augustina's vitals.

The Saint tapped them with one finger. "Don't be distressed; these will spike for a second when I connect. It's perfectly normal."

"Understood."

There was nothing else to say at that point, so St. Augustina got on with it. Setting the end of the cord at her neck port, she exhaled and focused on letting all of her unnecessary muscles go, completely supported by the chair itself. Then she slid the plug home.

She stood in Boyd's apartment staring at the blood splatters on the wall. A small line of it had been working on streaking down but had been frozen in place as St. Augustina called up the memory. She stood at the doorway, watching the techs and the unsharing detective frozen all around the victim's body.

St. Augustina stepped forward and tapped each being in turn. "Remove. Remove. Remove." They each vanished from the scenario. Soon, the space opened up, leaving only the victim on the ground, still covered by the sheet.

"Blessed Manasa, it's so... strange," Officer Papaqui said. The shadow avatar representing the goggles appeared next to her, it's "hands" gray instead of black to indicate the gloves.

"What is?" St. Augustina asked as she stepped down the hall to clear away the last tech who wielded the camera a few feet back.

"Well, I knew her. Not very well, but she was a person who I *knew*."

"Haven't had many people die in your life?" St. Augustina asked.

"Well ... no."

"You are very lucky," St. Augustina muttered, looking down the T-junction of the hallway.

"Where's the rest of the hallway?" Officer Papaqui asked. "Why can't I see anything?"

"Because I never made it this far into the apartment before they kicked me out. This is the borderline of the memory." She turned back to head to what she did remember.

"That is such—" And her officer started swearing in her coatl language again. St. Augustina thought she'd like to ask to learn some of these swears. They certainly sounded interesting, exotic, and very much on the nose.

Back in the living room, St. Augustina skimmed over the furniture and pictures on the wall. There was an entertainment

center with a couple of game consoles the Saint didn't recognize. She paced a slow circle around the room, trying to take everything in.

By contrast, Officer Papaqui went straight for the entertainment center that looked built into the wall. She immediately seized one of the drawers with her gray hand and pulled it open. "Huh," she said; she naturally saw nothing in it because St. Augustina had not looked within it. Then she closed the drawer and opened it again, and again, and again.

"What are you doing?" St. Augustina asked, mostly so she would stop trying.

"Oh, it's just... sometimes there are these drawers that change what's inside them every time you open and then shut them. I thought this was one of them, but I guess not."

"Really?" the Saint asked, intrigued.

"Oh, yes. All of our desks have at least one. It allows us to have more space."

"Hmm," St. Augustina said, making a mental note to go check out her own desk to figure out which one did that. "Well, speak up if you do see something you think might be pertinent to the case."

"What? Like these banners?" Officer Papaqui suddenly asked.

"Banners?" St. Augustina couldn't quite think of what she meant. Yet, she was right. Along the wall hung a couple of banners that sported strange runes stitched in gold thread. She dismissed the clipboard into the digital ether and spied the two cloth hangings with the runes on the wall.

St. Augustina took up a position in front of the nearest one and studied it, the shadow avatar doing the same. "What are you seeing?"

Her light gray fake hand brushed the front of one. "Well, those are vampiric runes, and Boyd was a Talent. Maybe there is something in that?"

The Saint narrowed her eyes at the banner. "You're going to have to explain the connection to me."

"Well, if you're a vampire and a Talent, the runes would help your magic manifest. Otherwise, they're just fancy cultural decorations. It's very similar to the way coatl runes work. My mother has them covering everything."

St. Augustina mulled that over. "But you think there might be something more to these runes that the corporate police might have missed?"

"Well," she could hear Officer Papaqui huff, "I was Boyd's partner for a time when I first started, so I know he had a Talent for placing what he called Aversion runes. He'd put them on his clothes and stuff all the time so that people wouldn't necessarily notice him. He said it made him more effective running security. He even put them on his lunchbox so Montgomery would stop raiding it. Even if he was actively looking for it, his eyes would sort of pass over the thing Boyd rune'd up."

The Saint put the pieces together. "Therefore, there could be some evidence in the apartment that Boyd hid behind an Aversion rune that anyone else would have not even noticed. Well done, Papaqui." She immediately initiated the jack-out command. The world around her collapsed into 3D pixels. The hot and cold rush made her wobbly on her feet as she tried to stand up too quickly from the chair before she had entirely settled into her body.

"What's going on? What's happening?" Officer Papaqui asked. She still stood next to the chair, turning left and right still looking through the goggles.

Before the Saint could pull the jack out of her neck, the chair shifted to sitting upright. The cord went taut, and since it was locked into the port, it almost yanked her off her feet. Gargling a cry, she quickly seized it and twisted it to break the magnetic seal so it would release. This was not dignified, and it was only luck that no one was witnessing it.

"Boss, I didn't break it, I swear," Officer Papaqui continued, clearly getting more panicked.

"It's fine. You can take the goggles off now," St. Augustina said. "We're done here."

The officer's crest lifted as she did as she was told. "But we barely looked?"

"What we need to find isn't going to be in my memories. We need to go to Boyd's apartment."

"You mean the closed crime scene, restricted to Paladins only?" the officer asked as she set the goggles next to the chair.

St. Augustina nibbled at her lower lip, sizing up her one and only officer. "You don't have to come with me."

Papaqui's crest pulsed. "I was going to say you have a lot more to lose if we got caught than I do, so I should be the one to go."

That answer surprised the Saint. "Thank you for your consideration," she said warily.

The coatl rewarded St. Augustina with one of her sharp-toothed smiles. "Like I said, I'm here to serve. I could break into the crime scene and take a look around. Then you can bail me out if I get caught."

St. Augustina stood up and moved to leave the room. "Don't take this the wrong way, but you've said yourself that you used to partner with Boyd. That is already a conflict of interest."

The coatl shrugged a shoulder. "Well ... but that's not really saying much. It was a small office to begin with, I mean, before you came. We all had to partner with each other at one time or another. Though..." Papaqui brightened up, "I did save Boyd's life once."

"That's not really helping with your case to not being a 'conflict of interest.' I would prefer if you just went home for tonight." St. Augustina said as she glanced up at the grotesque sitting, watching them above the door.

"But boss..."

"Go home, Officer. That's an order. I'll see you in the morning."

"But boss..."

"Have a good night, Officer Papaqui." St. Augustina didn't wait to hear anything further objections, simply let the office door fall shut with a resounding thump behind her.

CHAPTER 10

or St. Augustina, the night was just beginning. She walked a block away from the station, waiting as three trains rumbled by along the elevated tracks for good measure before she turned around the corner of the block and proceeded to hail a taxi. She grabbed the first one she spotted, and after a confirmation of the address, she passed her hand over the OmniSin reader in the back to prepay the ride. Fare covered, the driver left her alone to continue his phone conversation in a low, library tone, and that suited her just fine.

St. Augustina sat in the darkening cab, simply absorbing the silence and peace as the gray city slid past her window. So much of the Saint's existence had been at some level of alert. Dangers lurked around every corner. Every face could be an enemy with murderous intent, every ally a tool to be used and discarded. People like Officer Papaqui were so few and far between she had begun to believe that they were all dreams, but having spent the whole day with the coatl, she simply could not sense a dark-intended bone in the officer's body.

It had been nice.

But something still pinged as off to her, and the Saint didn't want to focus any more energy on being guarded around her when she had a crime scene to break into.

Too soon, the spell of the ride was over, and the driver double-parked the car on a snow-ridden street. The driver had barely given her enough room to open the door without clanking the nearby parked ones.

"Thank you, have a nice night," the driver said so automatically, she wondered if he was, in fact, an automaton.

"Thank you" was all she got out before the taxi drove off.

St. Augustina turned toward the apartment building. From the outside, it looked much of the same as it had two days ago, minus the police presence. She had intended to pick the front lock of the building's door, only to find someone had already blocked it open with a small square of roughed-up wood.

As she threaded her way around the steps to the third floor, noises echoed out into the stairwell from the busy lives of the dead woman's neighbors. Even through the doors, St. Augustina could hear the subdued tension they all wrestled with. A woman had been murdered mere feet from them, and they had not forgotten it yet. There was something honorable and right about that to St. Augustina, even as it was also sad.

Across the door on the third floor was an inelegant X of police line tape, dully yellow with its angry black writing. This time, the door was shut and locked, but a sweep from St. Augustina's augmentations confirmed no heat signatures of bodies on the other side and no camera equipment watching the door. This case was not a high priority for the corporate police department, obviously, if they wouldn't even spare a thirty-dollar camera to stand guard. She did a second sweep across the hallway wall since the stairs terminated on the third story, just to be sure. Then she saw why they hadn't bothered.

Magic laced the place. It was even stronger in the apartment behind her. A camera would have likely shorted out in that hallway. She had taken visual scans of the crime scene

before, but St. Augustina made a note in her augmented brain to remind her to look into an algorithm that ran an energy/electrical scan passively at the same time. If that hadn't been figured out yet, she would just need to make one up herself for future investigations. Maybe magic had an already existing solution that would work just as well?

Taking one last look and listen down the stairs, she knelt beside the door and focused on the lock. Despite the darkness, her augmentations popped out the lock clearly in her sight. It was a standard home improvement store setup. Not the cheapest lock, but a commercial one that could be easily broken with a determined kick. Except St. Augustina didn't want to make that much noise and didn't want to leave an obvious sign of her presence. Slipping her fingers into her inner pocket, she pulled out her bump-set, and just as she pulled out the tools to pick it, the door behind her opened.

The wedge of light blinded her with her night-vision active, but only for a moment before the augmentation automatically shut off. St. Augustina stayed still and coiled, preparing to strike whatever new enemy had found her. Then she heard a jingle of keys.

"You can use these if you like, Constable," an older woman's voice said, holding the small set of house keys out to her.

St. Augustina stood up and refocused on the woman before her. She was shorter, though most people were to St. Augustina, with permed silver hair and wrinkles covering her hands and features. Her sweater was a soft coral color that had been embroidered with the words, "Vampire Quilters Guild of Chicago," and a pair of needles underneath that were dripping drops of ruby-embroidered blood.

"Don't worry. I don't bite without permission," the older woman added before jingling the keys to be taken.

St. Augustina's hand grasped them, even if her mind hadn't caught up yet. "Thank you, Ms...?"

"Boyd. I was Gerald's aunt, Coraline Boyd. It is good to meet you, Constable St. Augustina," the woman said, a hint of an accent slipping into her English.

"How... How did you know it was me?" the constable asked, unable to not stumble on the question. She was completely flummoxed, feeling more like a kid who had been caught sneaking out than a bad-ass, cyber-enhanced investigator.

"I saw your picture in the Magic Guild newsletter when they formally announced your hire," she said simply. "I noticed you came by two days ago then the police were here."

"Yes, I'm... I'm working on getting jurisdiction back on your... nephew," the constable said, picking up her thoughts and trying to assemble them into coherent sentences.

Ms. Boyd nodded. "Good. That is good. That would be proper." She folded her arms. "Well? Are you going to open the door?" The vampire gave no sign of intending to go back into the apartment, so St. Augustina decided to act as if this was normal.

"I'm sorry for disturbing you."

"We could all hear you coming into the building. Vampires have very good hearing," Ms. Boyd said.

"I'll remember that."

"We are all very upset about what happened to Tiffany. She was a good girl," Ms. Boyd continued as the door swung open into the darkened apartment. Both women stared down at the taped outline of the body on the interior hallway floor, slashed across with light from Ms. Boyd's apartment and the shadow of their legs. Little number cards were set in different places where blood stained the ground down the hall, but those weren't what interested St. Augustina. She stepped under the cross of tape and entered the scene.

Ms. Boyd muttered something and crossed herself, then followed.

Another myth about vampires squashed, St. Augustina noted.

"The police called to tell us they released the scene, but they didn't bother to come clean up their mess. I wasn't going to say this to those corporate cops, but I will tell you that Gerry was always a troubled kid," Ms. Boyd said, crossing her arms again as she looked down at the tapped outline. "We all hoped that settling down with Tiffany was a good sign that he was getting better, but I didn't hold my breath."

"Why are you telling me this and not the other cops?" St. Augustina asked as she surveyed the living room again.

"You are one of us, aren't you?" Ms. Boyd said with a sniff. St. Augustina glanced back at her, but Ms. Boyd looked down at the ground, her face haunted. "You're all we got anyhow. I should have warned her about him. Don't know if it would have done any good, but ... he has too much of his father in him ... my brother. I know you're not supposed to judge a child by their parents, but sometimes, it is nature, no matter what the nurture."

"Boyd had a history of violence then?"

"It's tough for vampire kids. Too many misunderstand them and don't give them the chance they deserve," Ms. Boyd said bitterly. "It doesn't excuse anything, but I guess I just need to understand it in my own mind."

"You clearly think he did it."

The older woman nodded stiffly. "The whole community will turn on him now. Most already have." Ms. Boyd pinned St. Augustina with a weighted stare. "Violence against vampires is going to go up now. I just think you should know."

"We'll do our best to protect—"

"Don't make promises you can't keep. I am not a fool. I have lived too many years, and you are only just beginning. Others may have unreasonable expectations, but I am aware you will not be able to affect the real change we need for a few more years, if you ever get there at all. Not in time to make a real difference for my Gerald."

The vampire's candor spiked St. Augustina with a blade of shame. "I am going to do my best, Ms. Boyd. For everybody."

That earned her a shadow of a smile. "What is it you are looking for?"

St. Augustina returned to paying attention to her scans. So far, her augmentations listed very little in the way of new information. At least, from the living room.

"I don't know yet. Hopefully, something the corporate police would miss. Something they wouldn't think to see."

"You are investigating?"

"I have to do some political hoop jumping to get custody back so, until then, I might as well run a parallel investigation to help me build whatever case I'm going to need." She pointed at the banners wafting on the wall. "These for example. What do these runes mean?"

Ms. Boyd cast her eye over them. "They are just blessings. Protection, health, and wealth."

"Are they magical in any way?"

The vampire narrowed her eyes. "I'm not going to take offense at that because you wouldn't necessarily know better. They are blessings."

"Okay," St. Augustina said, taking the warning for what it was and backing off. Instead, she went to the drawers of the built-in entertainment center at the far end of the wall. She pulled open the one that Papaqui had in her simulation. Instead of a blank space, this time she saw various cords neatly wrapped up for various gaming systems. There were also incidental knickknacks and tools like spare batteries, a tiny screwdriver, and some zip ties. Slowly, St. Augustina shut the drawer, then opened it again. Still a draw full of cords and knickknacks. She shut it closed, counted to five, and then opened it a third time, just to be certain.

"What are you looking for?" Ms. Boyd asked.

"I heard there are magic drawers that open to different things when you do this," St. Augustina replied matter-of-factly.

"Oh, yes, a Wizard's Drawer. Over here," Ms. Boyd said and headed back out to the hall.

St. Augustina followed her, slipping her hands in her pockets as she did. The older woman led her to a side room that appeared to be an office that desperately needed an

organizer. Ms. Boyd clucked disparagingly at the mess as soon as she clicked on the light, muttering some African-sounding words under her breath as she shoved a box of more spilled-over papers out of her path so she could enter and go to a small cabinet in the corner behind the desk.

"I gave this to him for his graduation. Ai-ya-ya, I thought he would take better care of it. It was not cheap."

The older woman laid a hand on the front drawer of the cabinet. It was difficult to look at even though Ms. Boyd had her hand on it. Every time she tried, it was like her head was repelled away. The more times she tried, the more a headache threatened to form behind her eyeballs. Ms. Boyd didn't seem to notice St. Augustina's discomfort as she whistled, clucked her tongue and spoke another word that the Saint swore echoed with a tremor of power, even though nothing could echo in that densely packed room. A click sound came from the cabinet and the front drawer popped open. Once it did, it was actually possible to look at the drawer.

"You are a Talent?" St. Augustina asked, using the general term for all magic practitioners.

"I am a priestess of the daughters of Lamia, though I was also once an Obayifo," she intoned with the solemn self-assuredness all holy people seemed to have about their place in the world. "Many in my family have the gift, but not all, but that is not necessary for opening something such as this. I coded it for him precisely so he could open and use my present to him. Though not as a coaster!"

She plucked up a coffee cup that had been left, revealing an offensive ring on the wood, which his aunt wiped at disgustedly to no avail. Standing up, she cupped the offending ceramic in her hand and dance-stepped around the Saint.

"Excuse me, Constable. I will be right back. Please feel free to look as much as you need."

St. Augustina marveled at the vampire's trust. Following her invitation, the Saint sat down in the overly stuffed desk chair next to the cabinet and proceeded to slide the drawers open and closed. Sure enough, they switched contents with each pull. There were lots of folders and files in three of them. She skimmed through those, finding everything from renter's lease papers to the last six years of tax returns. Nothing of real interest or concern.

Then suddenly, the drawer stopped opening. It was like the whole thing had suddenly turned to stone and no matter how hard St. Augustina yanked, it would not be budged.

"Any luck, Constable?" Ms. Boyd asked as she came back into the room.

"Well, this was working, but now it stopped opening," St. Augustina said as she examined the drawer's seam to see if she had wedged or damaged it in any way.

"Let me see," the older woman said and came over to grasp the handle. When it didn't yield to her either, she clucked her tongue. "What is this? What is this?" Then the woman's eyes went ink black. The shift was so sudden and eerie that St. Augustina actually startled.

Ms. Boyd didn't seem to notice as she stared her void-colored eyes into the far middle distance. Uncanny whispers emanated from everywhere, and St. Augustina's skin got goosebumps, standing all the hairs straight up. She felt the urge to grab the gun she didn't carry anymore.

Then the cabinet snapped and popped as if protesting in pain. Ms. Boyd's brow quirked even as she continued to stare unblinking. The whispering became louder, more insistent.

"Gerry, what have you done?" the vampire asked, her voice hissing with power. Then the drawer popped straight out and banged her in the stomach. She blinked hard as a breath was kicked out of her. The blackness and whispers immediately stopped.

"Are you alright?" St. Augustina asked, bolting to her feet to catch the older woman.

Ms. Boyd laid her arm across her middle, bracing her other hand on the top of the cabinet, standing by will alone. Then she forced a gasping breath and cough.

The constable redirected her to the chair. "Can I get you anything?"

But the older woman waved a dismissive hand. "No, no," she gasped out. "It just knocked the wind from me. Just give me a moment to..." Then her words trailed away as her eyes popped open again. Her nose wrinkled, flaring uncannily wide. "Blood."

When she said the word, St. Augustina noticed it too. A tang, almost rotten scent of old blood. She turned to look down into the newly opened drawer, her jaw stiffening at what she saw. Several long strands of braided hair, coiled in circles, with dribbles of blood covering each.

"Trophies."

CHAPTER 11

Ms. Boyd's nose wrinkled as the strong smell of blood hit both their noses. Her eyes returned to their soulless blackness, and she took several steps back until she was at the door. Gripping the frame, her dark skin tinged greenish before she turned away.

"Ms. Boyd?" St. Augustina asked, standing up with every fiber of her being on alert.

"Do not concern yourself," Ms. Boyd growled, lifting a hand to her mouth. "I will not attack you, Constable."

"You didn't know anything about this?" the Saint asked.

The older vampire whirled. "Of course not!" Tears spilled from the blackened orbs of her eyes. St. Augustina caught a glimpse of her extended fangs before she covered them again with her hand, hiccupping a sob. "That poor child."

"Your nephew?"

Ms. Boyd looked away, her face a picture of anguish. "Tiffany. She said she had something to show me, to ask me

about. I... I forgot. She thought it was some sort of vampiric tradition."

"Is it?"

Anger flashed now, but Ms. Boyd's eyes cleared to reveal her human-like irises. Or more like they dilated back to a normal size, the pupil apparently capable of opening up until it filled the whole eye, creating the black eye every other living being feared. Her canines retreated as well, replaced by anger.

"Of course not! We are not as bloodthirsty as all you... you fangless believe!"

St. Augustina held up her hands in a placating gesture, and the vampire turned away again, collecting herself.

"Please forgive me, Constable. It is very dangerous for our kind to show any anger."

"It is alright, Ms. Boyd. I understand that this is all very upsetting."

The woman smiled bitterly. "You do *not* understand. This will spell much harm and death for my people. Despite the propaganda against us, we are just like any other living beings. We have our geniuses, our kindnesses, our good and our bad... But you know us for our psychopaths, not our doctors or teachers."

St. Augustina didn't know what to say to that, so she didn't even try. "Ms. Boyd, I would like to ask you to go into the other room while I complete my investigation. For your own sake," she said as gently as possible, with all the sympathy her voice could muster.

Ms. Boyd seemed to hear it. She nodded once and pulled her grief and despair back behind a stolid mask, the kind the Saint herself was all too familiar with on her own face. Once the vampire was gone, St. Augustina switched back to business.

She reached into one of the hidden inner pockets of her coat and removed a handful of evidence bags and a set of gloves. After observing everything to make her digital record, she bagged and tagged each item within the drawer. Then ran her fingers up, down, and around to be sure she had found every secret it contained. Storing her samples made that inner pocket bulge, but the lining would keep them all safe from contamination. Then she searched the rest of the room, going over everything to be sure, but she found nothing else. It took over an hour, and all the while Ms. Boyd stayed away.

Just as she was about to call out to the vampire that she had finished a bang snapped her attention. Shouts from angry voices came from the hallway: then there was a crash of wood splitting. St. Augustina sprang into action, dashing down the darkened hall toward the door that Ms. Boyd must have partially closed, but not latched. A sliver of wavering light and the grunts of bodies moving got louder as she whipped the door open to see the backs of several uniformed people moving into Ms. Boyd's apartment.

The last one heading in didn't know what grabbed him.

St. Augustina seized the back of his coat. He dropped to the ground onto his butt so that his head was at her waist height. Her internal computer formulated the right amount of electricity to divert into her hand as she struck. That one precise shock from her hand to the base of his skull knocked him out.

The next opponent barely turned back when she thrust her hand into his chin. Then her arm snaked through and around his neck, applying pressure to his windpipe. While his hands automatically grabbed at the immediate threat, she backpedaled him out the door. Once he cleared, the calibration completed so that she could non-lethally shock him like his fellow.

The rest of them were well inside the apartment, completely heedless of what was happening outside.

Men's voices bellowed violently. A woman cried out in pain. A bang, a crash.

St. Augustina sped through the door, shedding her coat as she went. She was in an apartment, a mirror opposite of the one she just left. Two men had pinned Ms. Boyd against the wall. Glass strewn about their feet. They were pressing so hard; her face was indented into the wall. Slurs and curses.

St. Augustina kicked down on the nearest one's knee, forcing it to bend to the ground. She didn't dare use the taser this time in case the shock conducted through to Ms. Boyd. The vampire's attacker still hadn't let go as his knee hit the ground, so she punched his accessible head. The impact snapped his skull too far to one side. He dropped defenseless just as the other one holding Ms. Boyd startled. He remained frozen where he was, torn between releasing his captive and defending his compatriot.

Another figure, the one brandishing a gun, appeared down the hall.

"Hands on your head!" the armed man shouted as he pointed his piece straight at her.

St. Augustina's augmentations increased her speed. Even as the gunman raised his weapon, she shifted. She punched the heel of her hand up into the second man holding Ms. Boyd. She then pulled on Ms. Boyd's arm. They both leaped through the open doorway into the living room just to the left of the door. When the gunshots fired, they buried into the wall where St. Augustina's head had been. Plastic chunks spat everywhere.

Ms. Boyd screamed. Her eyes had gone completely black again, and her fangs filled her mouth in a defensive response, but the vampire only dropped to a crouch covering her head with her hands. Blood streaked down her face from her nose, and one eye was bright red and clearly going to swell.

"Where's the bloodsucker!?" one of the men in the hall bellowed.

"She went around the corner!" another bellowed back. "There's another one!"

"Is F alright?" the first replied.

St. Augustina took their momentary confusion to align herself with the edge of the entryway. "This is Constable St. Augustina of the Magic Guild Authority! Identify yourselves!"

There was a long, weighted pause.

"What the fuck is she talking about?" one of the men hissed.

CHAPTER II

"This is the ... Paladin CPD. You will put down your weapons and come out with your hands up," the other man responded. He said it like it was rote, but the hesitation was odd. "You are aiding and abetting a criminal investigation."

"That's not what aiding and abetting means," St. Augustina countered, "which makes me doubt you are who you claim to be. Now, I will give you ten seconds to put down your arms and put *your* hands on your *own* damn heads before I—"

"Do as she says, or she'll kill you before you pull the next trigger," a new voice said from the doorway. "And I won't lift a damn finger to do anything about it if you're going to be that stupid."

Bold and as unconcerned as he could be, a tall, blonde man entered. He bent down at the doorway to retrieve St. Augustina's coat, laying it over his arm like a trained butler before turning a boy-next-door smile over at its owner. "Hello, St. Augustina. It's nice to see you again."

"St. Dominic," she acknowledged as she straightened herself in the presence of the other Saint. This changed everything. "And what institution would have an interest in harassing innocent old ladies?"

He cocked an eyebrow at her that spoke volumes and implied she would need to wait for the details until he had cleared the room. "I said, holster those guns *now*. This operation is more than adequately cocked up." He gestured with his head to the hallway. "Take care of J and T. They're going to need some medical attention. Possibly some counseling."

She could hear the tension in the unseen lackeys, but St. Dominic stared them both down. Then she heard the telltale clicks of safeties re-engaging followed by the swish of metal on leather, weapons being put back into their holsters. Sounds only enhanced ears would catch. St. Dominic shifted casually to the side, a move that tactically placed himself between his men and St. Augustina, though whether it was to guard them or her and Ms. Boyd, she couldn't say.

Once they were gone, St. Dominic shut the door before turning and offering St. Augustina her coat. "I thank you for your restraint," he said.

She took the coat, it was hers after all, and slipped it back on. "I don't know what restraint you think that was."

"You could have killed them, and you didn't."

She sniffed at that. "I don't kill unless I have to, and we weren't there yet."

He nodded at that. "Still, it saves me on a load of paperwork and condolence letters I don't mean."

The trouble was, she knew that was true. St. Dominic was as cold, and as ideal a Saint, as they come. Something St. Augustina pretended at but could never really be.

"You're welcome," she lied.

His eyes drifted over her shoulder to regard Ms. Boyd, and St. Augustina took a slight step into his line of sight to break that gaze. He chuckled then drifted it pointedly down to St. Augustina's constable badge hanging from its chain around her neck.

"I guess we don't get to pick our assignments, but I would love to find out how the Magic Guild managed to pull your acquisition off."

"And who are *you* working for these days, St. Dom?"

His smile grew terse. "I'm on loan to Paladin CPD. I understand there has been a vampire murder against a Kodiak employee that, apparently, someone cared enough about to want me transferred in as a detective." He pulled his own shield on its chain out from within the folds of his coat to show her. "I saw your name on the report. Are you claiming jurisdiction?"

"Of course, I am."

"You got a way to enforce that?"

He knew she didn't, but there was a real question in his eyes. He had run the calculations.

"You know me," she stated, and an understanding passed between them. If she didn't have it yet, she would have it soon.

She knew the calculation he would run now; how much was it worth it to counter whatever she might have planned?

He sighed and rubbed his forehead. "And just when I thought this would be an easy assignment."

"It still can be," she offered.

He shook his head. "No, no. You know me. I gotta win."

Now, it was her turn to internally curse. He shrugged and reopened the door.

"Who knows? You might even beat me. Wouldn't that be funny?" he added.

"A laugh riot," she promised, letting a decent amount of unamused threat slip into her voice.

He didn't respond. He simply shut the door.

She didn't move a muscle as her enhanced hearing listened with every fiber: real and synthetic. With a triple blink, she activated her eye augmentations and selected the heat signature reader. The wall grayed out in her vision, and on the other side, she saw the heat spectrum glow of two bodies that seemed to carry a third down the stairs. A fourth stood at the top to supervise them with the silver sparks that indicated active augmentations. Like herself, St. Dominic had opted for the physical augmentations at his joints and at the base of his spine to control his chemical responses. In a toe-to-toe fight between them, the outcome was not guaranteed.

"Are they—?" Ms. Boyd started, but St. Augustina held up a hand to shush her.

She watched the spectral-colored figure of St. Dominic turn back toward the door for a second, then plod down the steps, following his retreating men. She waited a full ten seconds, even as Ms. Boyd fell apart behind, collapsing onto the floor in a pile of shaken-up tears.

"This was my home," she cried. "They came into my home!"

St. Augustina went to the window on the other side of the living room to look down at the officers as they filed out the front door into the courtyard. As if feeling her gaze, St. Dominic turned up to look at her in the dying winter light, the

snow illuminating him with shadows from below. He smirked, and she tightened her fist against the sill.

"I told you. I told you they will come for us. We will all pay for what my nephew has done," Ms. Boyd said, her voice going flat as the tears dried on her face and moved to thicken her throat.

"Do you have somewhere else you can go?" St. Augustina asked, still watching as St. Dominic climbed into an unmarked car, which pulled out as soon as his door was shut. A second car followed his.

"Go? Where? This whole building is full of vampires. If I were to go anywhere, it would be here."

"Then stay with someone else here tonight, just not in your apartment," St. Augustina said as she pulled down the shade on the window.

"What good will that do? If they want to find me, they will find me and hurt everyone else in their way to get what they want."

"They already have what they want, and they know I'm watching." St. Augustina turned back to the woman still sitting like a broken doll on the floor. Her eyes were also still completely black, but this time it reminded the Saint of a small mouse instead of a monster.

Sighing, she offered her hand to help Ms. Boyd up. "It's going to be alright: I promise."

Ms. Boyd picked herself up off the floor, waving away St. Augustina's hand. "Do not lie to me, Constable. I am getting too old for that. There is nothing that can be done. This too shall pass."

"What did they say to you when they showed up?" St. Augustina asked.

"They didn't say much. Just 'Open up,' and 'Show us your hands.'" Ms. Boyd tossed her own hands in a show of exaggeration.

"They didn't announce themselves or what department they were with?"

CHAPTER 11

"No, nothing, just guns, guns, guns." Ms. Boyd paused as she set herself on the arm of her sofa. "What does that mean?"

"This job was off the books. They aren't here in an official capacity, and they've brought a Saint in on the job. I think I need to figure out why."

CHAPTER 12

The hour had marched past noon by the time St. Augustina returned to the Guard office. She waited in her car all night outside Ms. Boyd's apartment building, keeping watch to be sure that St. Dominic or anyone else for that matter, didn't show up again. Only when the building started waking up did she head home and get some sleep. She was the boss after all. Who did she have to report to?

Still, it occurred to her as she brushed her teeth that morning: the fact that there were no calls was because she had never given Papaqui one of the business cards she handed out to everyone else freely.

With that in mind, she stopped at the amazing 24-hour coffee shop in the Magic Guild building. They provided her a tray and three coffees along with all the sugars and creams she wanted occupying the fourth spot. She wasn't sure if Officer Papaqui would still be at the office, but sure enough, the coatl sat curled up asleep at her desk, waiting for her.

Not having the heart to wake her yet, St. Augustina set the tray of coffees on one of the empty desks next to her and began preparing her own with her highly coveted hazelnut creamer, the one thing other than her uneaten lunch in the cold drawer. It apparently had a preservation spell on it as well because, when she checked on the take-out tray, the quiche and flourless chocolate cake looked as pristine as the day she purchased it.

"Magic does seem to have its advantages over tech," she muttered softly to herself and went back into the main room to imbibe.

The first sip of her coffee was lava hot and supremely delicious. She imagined it burning away her fatigue even if such a thing wasn't truly possible. Once she had taken two more gulps, she set her cup down and picked up one of the two remaining containers.

"This one is for you," she said to the grotesque staring at her from its shelf, if "it" was the right pronoun for the creature. Just as Officer Papaqui had insisted, the thing continued to act like an inanimate object; didn't react or blink or even twitch.

She pushed away the sensation of feeling stupid and plucked up a creamer and a packet of sugar. Even though St. Augustina was artificially tall, thanks to the augmentations in her joints, she didn't quite reach all the way to the shelf the grotesque sat upon, so she had to haul a chair underneath.

"Here you go," she said as she slid her offering up onto the shelf along with the things to dress it. "I don't know if you like cream or sugar, but if you let me know how you take it, I will make sure I bring that."

Again, the grotesque didn't react, only continued staring. St. Augustina shrugged and clambered down but failed to do so quietly. The chair slid across the floor as her foot hit the ground and the officer "on duty" sat bolt upright, crest at full alert.

"Oh! Ma'am! You're back. I mean, you're here." Scrubbing her hands over her face, the coatl yawned.

"I'm surprised *you're* still here. It's past noon."

"Well, I thought it best to stay by the phone in case I'm needed."

"Thank you for the vote of confidence," St. Augustina grimaced and handed the final coffee to Papaqui with the remaining creamers and sugars. Then she took out one of her business cards and set it on top, just as her officer moved to take her cup.

"Oh!" she said, blinking her secondary eyelid at it.

"So you can call me."

"Oh, yes, yes ma'am," the officer said and slipped the card into her slacks pocket, but then her crest flexed, "but I already knew where you were."

St. Augustina paused. "You did?"

"Well yes, you know, because of the map," she gestured toward the back wall. Looking at it all, St. Augustina saw a series of cubed panels lined up perfectly equidistant from each other, like some minimalist art installation. She hadn't really paid it much mind other than to note how dusty it was. "What map?"

"Oh, here," Officer Papaqui popped up from her chair and scurried over to the wall. "Display the whole building."

A clack sound rolled through the wall, and each of the squares shifted and shimmied to life. Then the squares divided, separating into smaller squares, then morphed as if they were soft clay instead of wood. They moved about the wall, sliding and grinding into nine smaller reliefs.

"These are ... each floor of the building," St. Augustina said as she strolled over to the living map.

"Yup," Officer Papaqui confirmed, then gestured up to the grotesque above the door. "Everything those things see are transferred to this map. She then tapped one of the wooden sections. "This here is our office." The wooden pieces froze, then reversed, shifting and morphing to form a large single square, but this one was a detailed relief of the actual office they

stood in, including two small figures staring at the backwall. Across, in the actual space, the grotesques eyes glowed green.

"See, what it sees, this map will show," the coatl said, as she backed away a few feet from the wall. Sure enough, the wood blocks shifted to show the figure shifting back from the wall.

"This is interesting," the Saint acknowledged.

"It can do the whole city." Officer Papaqui tapped one of the boards twice quickly, waited a moment, then twice quickly again. The clacks filled the room as the wall shifted into an overhead grid map of the entire city of Chicago.

Pleased, Officer Papaqui gave a trilling whistle then said, "Reveal location of Constable St. Augustina. Over the representation of the Magic Guild building, a single block switched between white and black. "And that's you. This map can detect anyone who works for the Magic Guild, anywhere in the city." She double-tapped this time on the "blinking" spot, and the map rearranged to show the interior of their office once more. "So I knew where you were this whole time."

"That is ... amazing," St. Augustina said, wishing there was another, less over-used word for it, but there simply wasn't.

"Now, just so you know, we only get this level of detail in the places that the grotesques can see, so you don't get this throughout the rest of the city, but in our controlled neighborhoods..." She tapped out a rhythm on the boards, and they reformed to the city, then she double-tapped onto the neighborhood labeled "Lincoln Square." "And there we are, a perfect map of Lincoln Square."

"But I didn't see any gargoyles or grotesques at Lincoln Square when we were there," the Saint noted.

"What did you think the cows were for?" Officer Papaqui went back to her desk to pick up her coffee to gulp it down while St. Augustina continued to study the map. "Tap it three times quickly and twice slowly, and it'll show you where all the security grotesques are on the map."

She did, and it did, doing the same thing as before, flipping between a light block and a dark block where the cows were all positioned. "Is there anything else it can show me?" she asked.

"Uh, yeah, we can also get a layout of all the transfer doors for the whole city, and there is also supposed to be a command to show which ones connect to which ones, but I don't know that one off the top of my head. That book hanging from the cord there has all the map commands in it."

Sure enough, suspended from a cord on a hook in the wall was a roughed-up, red-covered book with much-abused pages leafing out. She picked it up to glance at where the book fell naturally open and saw a list of neatly printed knock commands for various things the map could do. Some had been crossed out and new ones written in, which told her that the whole thing was also... programmable, for lack of a better word. Finding the command to show all the transfer doors, she knocked it into the map. More flickering bits of wood.

"And there are hundreds of these doors," St. Augustina muttered with a sigh. "And only one of me."

"Well?" Officer Papaqui asked as she popped off the top of her cup and poured in the remaining creamers and half a packet of sugar into what remained of her coffee. "Pretty cool, right?"

Two of me, St. Augustina corrected mentally. Instead of answering her officer's question, she glanced down into the book and found the command to locate a specific person. She imitated the whistle and then said "Officer Boyd."

This time the map didn't respond.

"Oh, no, you won't find him that way anymore. He declared out loud to the map that he doesn't work here anymore, which is the command to break the spell for you. Aside from that command, the only other way to break it is if you're dead."

"This is very useful," St. Augustina acknowledged as she unhooked the book from its hook. "I'll have to study these commands and see what else we can do with it." She glanced up at the office grotesque, but he continued to stare unmoving, his coffee untouched.

"Did you discover anything from the crime scene last night?" Officer Papaqui asked, drawing her attention back.

"Oh... Yeah... Yes, 1 did." St. Augustina hesitated. It felt wrong to just pull out the evidence she had taken in such a large, open room, but they were the only ones there, and the grotesque wasn't talking.

She slipped the plastic bags out of her large inner pocket and set them on the desk before her officer. With a shudder of feathers, Officer Papaqui narrowed her eyes at the bags before picking one up to smooth the plastic so she could see clearer within.

"What are these?" she asked, her voice tremoring, like she dreaded the answer.

St. Augustina blew out a breath. "I... 1 didn't get a chance to ask, but 1 found them in Boyd's apartment." She pointed at the bag. "That's definitely blood, and this is made of bone. I'm not sure what everything else is. I have programs that can confirm the first two, but a deeper chemical analysis would require a forensic specialist and better equipment. What 1 did get from the preliminary blood samples is that they are all different species."

While she didn't drop the bag at the gristly informa-tion, Officer Papaqui did set it down quickly. "Manasa," she muttered. "In Boyd's apartment?"

St. Augustina nodded. "Hidden behind some vampiric runes just like you said. Even knowing what to look for, it had been difficult to focus on the drawer. And then the drawer itself was further enchanted to switch many times. No mun-dane police person would have just 'found' it."

"So will that help your petition to get the case moved to our jurisdiction?"

The Saint shrugged. "We'll see, but it can't hurt. 1 obtained this evidence lawfully."

The officer continued to stare at the bundles for a long second, flicking her tongue as if she could taste the air around for more clues. "If there are fingerprints on the bundles then..."

"We're going to need to find a forensic firm that will run this for us," St. Augustina concluded, taking another longer drink from her coffee.

"There *is* a forensic lab that the Guard uses. We don't get things that need it very often, but let me make a call first. Boyd was the one who had the connection at the office."

"Please do. Does this office have a safe or an evidence locker where we can store this safely?"

"Uh, yes." Officer Papaqui went over to the bookshelf filled with tomes behind glass. Setting her fingers against a small crystal in the frame, Officer Papaqui muttered something St. Augustina didn't quite make out. The door popped open. Within, she selected one of the tomes: a leather volume bound in blue leather and filled with thick sheets of paper. Pulling it from the topmost shelf, she set it on a stand nearby, obviously placed for that exact purpose. The book had several bookmarks sticking out of the bottom, stuck at various intervals throughout. The officer plucked up the one near the end of the book and used it to open the pages before flipping forward to a blank page.

"What are you doing?" St. Augustina asked, stepping up to watch.

"This is how we secure documents and evidence." She set the bags on the page and then shut the book, pulling her finger out of the way at the last second.

St. Augustina leaned in further trying to understand what had happened. The edges of the pages lay undisturbed for having an object shoved in between them.

To continue her demonstration, Officer Papaqui opened the book wide once more with her snake's grin. On the surface of the left side page was a drawing of the evidence bag and its gristly contents. The drawing was uncanny as if someone had inked a photo-realistic copy of the object, only without

color. The Saint slid a finger over the surface, but all she felt was smooth paper.

"How do we get it back?" she asked, marveling.

"You put your hand over the image and sort of ... will it into your hand," Papaqui said, closing the book once more to reveal a sheet of paper taped to the stand's surface. She turned the book to face the spine toward herself and plucked up a pen hanging from a chain attached to the top of the book stand. Jotting down the numbers on the spine onto the sheet, she finished by signing her name under the check-in column.

"Really? That simple? No magic words required?" St. Augustina asked, gesturing for the tome, which Officer Papaqui passed to her easily. The tome felt heavy, but no more than a good library book would. She started to flip open the pages, seeing countless realistic drawings of countless objects.

"Anyone can do it, no Talent needed. The magic is already in the book."

The Saint flipped through the pages again looking at the various objects. She noticed at the top of each page were labels for the objects and names of whom they belonged to. "Fluffy handcuffs, Dennis Quarterly. Peridot necklace, Cora Timon. Schrodinger's Cat, unknown. Enslavement rings?"

"Oh, yes, those are very dangerous," Papaqui said. "We get all kinds of illegal contraband in here like that." She glances at the page. "These were seized... oh that's right. These are going to need to be returned to the owner. Looks like Montgomery didn't take care of that before he left."

"Returned to the owner? How do you mean?"

"These were taken off a wizard suffering from dementia. He apparently was in between caregivers, his daughters I think, and they were passing the master ring between them, and I guess there was some miscommunication or something? He got a hold of it somehow and went off wandering down Lake Shore Drive before we found him. He wasn't hurt, but without the rings he could have been a danger to himself and others."

"So there is a legal application for something like this?"

"Oh, yeah, definitely. In this case, medical. When he was lucid, he signed a medical waver to entrust the master ring to his daughters so that he could continue to receive hospice care at home. I'll make a call right now and get this case sorted."

St. Augustina returned the book, and Officer Papaqui put it back up behind the glass.

"The glass is enchanted as well not to break, and the key will only turn for an active member of the Guard." She attempted to demonstrate by turning the key, but much to Officer Papaqui's consternation, it didn't turn. "At least when it freaking wants to!"

St. Augustina smirked to herself. She would love to see St. Dominic try to hack a system like that. "Here let me try," the Saint offered, and she withdrew the skeleton key, blew on the teeth, then reinserted it. It turned easily. "My grandmother had a cabinet like this. It's what she'd do to get it to work."

Officer Papaqui shot the cabinet an annoyed glare. "This is also what we do with all of our documents," she added. She returned to her desk to hold up another volume from a stack of five, this one a large tan-colored tome and held it out to St. Augustina. "While you were gone, I pulled out all of Boyd's case records. I thought maybe there would be something within them that could help us."

"That's excellent thinking," St. Augustina praised as she came over to take the magical book from her. Opening it, she saw the pages filled with writing and photos. "So everything is kept within books?"

"Yes, and this works the same way as the evidence books. Just lay your hand over the page and will it into your hand."

Except when St. Augustina did, nothing happened. "What am I doing wrong?"

Officer Papaqui worried her lip. "Um, maybe... do you believe it's going to happen?"

The Saint furrowed her brows, then shrugged one shoulder. "No, not really, I suppose," she admitted.

"Yeah, that's the thing about magic. At least, that was what my training officer told me. Magic is more about intention than anything else, so if you believe in it, it'll believe in you."

"Interesting perspective," St. Augustina noted and returned her hand to the surface of the page.

Why would this be any different from manipulating an object made of light? Those seemed as real to her as anything else in this world. This time, her fingers pulled across the page, lifting up a very different sheet of paper, white from the cream-colored surface. Looking at the report that had manifested in her hands, St. Augustina laid it back down on the surface and closed the book. Sure enough, it had returned to the page. "This is quite extraordinary."

"Thank you," the officer said as if she could take credit for the book's creation. "We'll have to have one set up for you too now."

"That won't be necessary," St. Augustina said, tapping her temple. "Anything I see, I record with my augmentation, whether I notice it or not. Just like you saw when I showed you Boyd's apartment."

"Oh... I see." Officer Papaqui took up the next book on the stack. "The nice thing about this system is you don't have to pull out every report to read them. Just flip through." The coatl settled in her desk chair and laid the tome out before her. "Still isn't going to be easy if we don't know what we're looking for."

"This could wait until tomorrow," St. Augustina offered.

"Are you going to go home already?" her subordinate asked, meeting her eyes earnestly.

She thought for a moment about lying. "No," she admitted.

"It won't take as long if we're both at it," Officer Papaqui said and pulled a yellow legal pad toward herself waiting for notes. "The one you have in your hand there is the one when Boyd and I were partners. You know, so we don't have a conflict of interest."

The coatl cracked a smile, which was getting less uncanny every time she did it. Officer Papaqui sure smiled a lot, which the Saint couldn't stop from spreading to her own face.

"Alright," she agreed, pulling out the chair of the empty desk to the officer's right.

They had their work cut out for them.

CHAPTER 13

"**A**nything?" St. Augustina asked.

Officer Papaqui slapped closed her tome in a clear non-verbal answer of "no." "Okay, I might not be able to go on much longer," the officer admitted.

Sinking her fingers into the rock that was the back of her neck, St. Augustina was right there with her. Glancing up at the large clock next to the door, she sighed as she realized it was getting late. "Okay, how about we both take a late morning, and come back fresh tomorrow?"

"I've just got this last tome and then yeah, I'm for that," Officer Papaqui agreed, sliding the last of the stack toward herself.

As the Saint closed her own book, she turned the spine toward herself with a sigh.

Most of the cases she had read were fairly boring: public disturbances, petty vandalisms, and theft. Certainly nothing remotely more exciting than a couple of incidents of assault

and battery, and even those were more about black eyes than broken bones.

It was odd for a city this big.

"Hey, didn't you say you saved Boyd's life once?" St. Augustina asked, sitting up to the desk again while she jotted down that thought.

"Yeah." The officer nodded and arched her back until it audibly cracked.

"Where's that incident? Where's the report on that?"

"Oh, uh..." The coatl looked down at the mess of tomes and papers on both the desks before digging under St. Augustina's stack to pull a tome from the bottom. She checked the spine, running a finger underneath the year. "Here, this was it. Around June. Do you want me to get my report too?"

"Please." St. Augustina nodded and took the tome to open to the page that started June with the cloth bookmark marked with a large Ju.

While Officer Papaqui was at the glass shelf to retrieve her own case file tome, St. Augustina flicked through the pages quickly, recalling having seen these case files already. Papaqui returned to the desk, holding her own tome as she flipped through herself.

"Here it is," she said as she turned the book to offer to her superior.

"I'm not finding it in here," St. Augustina said frustratedly as she fingered the July bookmark as if it were at fault for her failure.

"What? That's impossible," Officer Papaqui said. They traded books.

"Well, see if you can find it. It is entirely possible I'm too brain-fried to see it."

St. Augustina scanned over Officer Papaqui's copy of the report, her eyes freezing halfway down. "Boyd was shot?"

"Uh, yeah. The human male in the domestic dispute pulled a gun on his troll girlfriend and fired while she was raging. Bastard later claimed he was afraid for his life, and he bought the gun to protect himself from her because she was stronger than him. But there were all these social media posts about how proud he was of his gun when he bought it the year before he started dating her. Boyd was determined to put that guy away for life. I think he only got fifteen years."

"So Boyd's injury wasn't that serious?"

"Oh, it was very serious. He almost didn't make it. Then he did."

St. Augustina skimmed over the details again, thinking about that.

"This can't be right!" Officer Papaqui declared, setting Boyd's book down onto the desk so she could lean over it. "Boyd was a meticulous record keeper... and, there is no way... I mean he was shot! Someone would have noticed if he hadn't put a report in for that! I mean, insurance would have needed it and workman's comp and all that."

Then a thought struck St. Augustina.

Reaching across the desk, she set Officer Papaqui's book aside and pulled the other back toward herself. With the flourish of a street magician, she called up her holodesk and created a digital wall in front of herself. With a few gestures, she called up a detection program. Opening the parameters menu, she typed in a few commands.

"What are you doing?" Officer Papaqui asked.

St. Augustina didn't answer yet, remaining focused, carefully reading again.

"Ma'am?"

"Give me a minute. I want to try something."

She continued to read, flipping the page to keep going. Then Officer Papaqui gasped, which broke the Saint's concentration. Looking up, she checked the light wall of her holodesk. Within a window, a line of text had appeared.

"Homicide," St. Augustina read out. She exchanged a shocked glance with Officer Papaqui. "Can you see that on this page?"

Officer Papaqui shook her head. "No."

"So his Aversion magic works on his reports too," St. Augustina concluded.

"How are you doing that?" Officer Papaqui asked, wafting her claws through the light wall, making it waver as they passed through.

"I've set up the program to detect when my eyes avoid anything in order to have what I'm not seeing harvested." She continued to scan her eyes over the pages, realizing she didn't actually need to read them to make the trick work.

"That... That's awesome!" Officer Papaqui cawed as more text appeared. She began reading while St. Augustina continued her scan. As the officer's eyes passed back and forth over the text, her feather crest drooped more and more, and what St. Augustina could only describe as a sick look came over her face as the scaled surface of the coatl's face seemed to shift from a green tinge to yellow.

St. Augustina didn't ask until she had finished the entire tome, sitting back in her chair to take in Officer Papaqui's reactions. "What is it?"

"They are all murders or missing person cases. So many... too many..." she said, her body moving stiffly. The officer picked up her notebook and made tick marks. *She's counting*, St. Augustina realized.

"How many?"

"Six. All in the last three years. Several should have been forwarded on to the corresponding corporate jurisdictions, but there are no confirmations here to verify that they were."

"The victims just disappeared from the world."

"And since we've had no supervising authority in the last four years..." Officer Papaqui looked pained and sat down in her chair too hard like her legs had been about to give out from under her.

St. Augustina didn't comment on it, passing her own eyes over the now-readable text. "Is there a pattern to the races of the victims?"

"All different kinds," Officer Papaqui confirmed.

"Then we need to see if any of these people match with the evidence we've collected," St. Augustina concluded, "and I need to get Morlock on the phone."

"What for?"

"This all has a feeling of ritual about it, but he would have more insight—" she started to say, but a yawn cut her off. The effects of the coffee had long worn off and while her augmentations could keep her upright if she needed, St. Augustina had to recognize that forcing them to do so when doing simpler things like getting some sleep would stave off long-term problems. Standing up, she glanced at the holographic clock in her holodesk. 9:32 PM. "Morlock keeps daytime hours, correct?"

"Actually, he does a sort of half-day/half-night thing. He probably opened shop hours ago. He rarely opens for business before 3 PM."

St. Augustina nodded since that made perfect sense. She gathered up the tomes and Officer Papaqui moved to help her. "Did you hear back from your connection at the lab?"

"I doubt we will until tomorrow."

"Then let's get that sorted before we talk to Morlock. We need to lock these all up and get some sleep ourselves. Meet back here tomorrow?"

"I can do that," Officer Papaqui confirmed, barely suppressing her own yawn as she shut the door on the tomes.

They said little else as they gathered up their coats and tossed the coffee cups into the bin. Officer Papaqui exited first, with St. Augustina gesturing away the light crystals to off as she had been shown. Just before she passed under the doorway and out, something dropped on top of her head and bounced into the hallway.

It was an empty coffee cup. Picking it up, she opened the inside and saw the garbage from a creamer and a packet of sugar stuffed inside.

"Okay then."

CHAPTER 14

Morlock stared at the baggies with haunted eyes, his flask at the ready. He seemed to be able to hold his guts in check if he didn't think too hard about what they were made of. When she managed to get him on the phone, it had surprised St. Augustina that he had offered to come into the office himself, instead of her going to him with her evidence. Judging by his expression, she could now understand why.

"Has anybody else seen these?" he finally asked, still not breaking his gaze from them.

"No, I only found it the other night. We had planned to send them out for testing, but we're having difficulty getting a lab to take us on. Do you know what they are?" St. Augustina asked, folding her arms across her chest as she leaned against an empty desk.

Morlock released a held breath in a tired sigh that seemed generations old. "Yes, though I am probably one of a handful of people who could actually identify these things on sight. They are 'Farmecul pentru a lega strigoii,'" he said suddenly

speaking a language St. Augustina's implants struggled to immediately translate. "Charm to bind the undead," he added in English, just as her implants caught up, displaying the same words within her sight.

Officer Papaqui stepped beside Morlock, offering him a cup of freshly brewed coffee from a crystal-run brewer she had brought from home.

He took it but didn't make any move to sip. "Where did you find these?"

"In a cabinet, in Boyd's apartment. Inside a drawer enchanted to both be not noticed and difficult to open."

"How did you find it then?" Morlock asked, finally looking at St. Augustina.

"Boyd's aunt helped me. She also let me in. I understand the lease for the apartment is in her name."

Morlock sniffed at that. "Well, that clears up any legal grayness we would have otherwise had, if she aided in the search."

The Saint nodded. "Do you think this will be enough to qualify having Boyd moved to Magic Guild jurisdiction?"

"Oh, gods yes. If this doesn't, then nothing will and we are in more trouble than we all realized," Morlock said and finally quaffed a deep drink of his office-provided coffee.

St. Augustina straightened. "Then we have everything we need to go to the judge and get the transfer order."

"Who is the judge?" Morlock asked.

"Alonzo Alvarez-Hughes."

Morlock seemed to roll that around in his head a moment. "*I* can go to the judge and request the transfer on behalf of my client."

"You're Boyd's lawyer?" St. Augustina asked, surprised.

"No, not yet, not yet." He met her gaze with his own, and then he reached into an inner pocket of his jacket and withdrew a business card. "But if I was, a plea from a member of the Magic Guild for Magic Guild protection will get the transfer done faster than one from the Magic Guild, especially.... I can

request that it be sealed." He handed her the card. "Give this to Boyd. Have him call me. I will take his case."

St. Augustina secured it in her own pocket. "Ethics issues?"

"It's not soliciting if someone were to give him my card," Morlock confirmed. "I'll be waiting.

The constable pushed through the spinning door into the main lobby of the police station. It felt very corporate and familiar, from the twitchy lights above to the industrial carpet. This office obviously had money; however, as everything was laid out with clear glass-like walls in between each desk, it made the place feel more open. She could even spot a mid-level cappuccino machine in the break room.

She felt a breath of cold air continue to blow on the back of her neck as Officer Papaqui passed through the spinning doors behind her.

St. Augustina plastered on a professional, if stiff, smile and approached the desk where a police officer, her bottle-blonde hair in a bun, looked at her with stoic expectation. "Can I help you?" she asked, firmly, as if St. Augustina's mere presence was wasting her time.

Fun.

"Constable St. Augustina to meet with Head Detective St. Dominic," she said, lifting her badge for the woman to see. The officer's eyes narrowed at it, and St. Augustina let her have a good long look at the Magic Guild emblem and hazelnuts.

Finally, the police officer picked up a phone. "One moment please."

St. Augustina let the shield drop back under her open coat and slipped her hands into the pockets to finger the half bottles of water she carried at the bottom. With a casual ease, she looked around the space while the woman made her call. Her eyes were activated, one blue and one yellow,

which made a suit-wearing detective nearby pause to stare at her for the length of a hiccup. She didn't care. St. Dominic would know she would do this, so nothing really juicy would just be lying out, but you never know. Sometimes people get lucky, no one can cover every base. And it was best to act as St. Dominic expected.

The landline phone clacked back into its cradle, pulling St. Augustina's attention back to the front desk officer. The woman opened her mouth to speak, then her own eyes widened at the sight of St. Augustina's eyes. It took her a longer hiccup to recover. "Detective Dominic is unavailable right now."

St. Augustina's jaw tightened at the drop of the Saint honorific from St. Dom's name, but it told her that his status as a Saint was being kept under wraps. This was in fact a temporary assignment for him then. Even the fact that these people didn't understand the designation felt like a message to her from him. It had always seemed like hubris to her, to have such an open secret like that attached to her name, but marketing for a Saint's services seemed to outweigh the risks of exposure. The upper echelons certainly loved their open secrets.

None of that solved her current situation.

"But—" Officer Papaqui started to say as she pulled down the hood from her head, releasing her crest as it rose in colorful irritation. The officer's eyes went indiscreetly wide at that.

St. Augustina raised a gloved hand, silencing her officer. "I have a right to see Mr. Boyd in my capacity as—"

"Absolutely, ma'am," the officer interrupted, coming back to herself. "I have been instructed to give you access to him for one hour in interrogation room three." As she spoke, the officer pulled out a pre-stapled stack of papers, turning it toward St. Augustina to indicate pre-x'ed lines. "Sign here, here, initial, sign."

The Saint did so and soon found herself led to a standard interrogation room with three blank walls, a glass mirror that was actually a window, and a plain table with two chairs. A bar was fixed to the top of the table at one end, and St. Augustina's augmentations noted the darker stains, even with the smell of bleach in the air.

At this point, Officer Papaqui had divulged herself of her coat, draping it over one arm, but she remained in her snow pants and polo with its Magic Guild Guard emblem stamped over the right breast pocket side. Otherwise, she looked very much at ease.

St. Augustina took the chair opposite the bar and sat to wait. Two people were watching her from the other side of the mirror-like glass; she could see their heat signatures with her augmentations. Out of curiosity, she allowed her internal computer to check for network links, debating on whether it would be worth the risk to open up her consciousness to it. Most network techs wouldn't even notice it as human-to-computer interfaces were still new and, in a lot of ways, mostly whispered rumor, which was a big edge for Saints. Normally.

But a Saint was here and in charge and had let her in through the front door. She decided against the exposure.

Finally, the door opened, and two pairs of officers walked a fifth man into the room. Chains chinked and clinked as the orange-clad man shuffled in. He also wore a pair of manacles linked by a chain between his feet and wrists, then joined in the middle of each. He also had a gag around his face with a small clinking lock binding it to the side of his head. The gag had a window with a grill in front of it, a row of five squares, just large enough for air and a straw to pass through. It looked crusty around the window, and St. Augustina imagined that was how they were keeping him alive.

Officer Papaqui gasped at the sight. "By the Holy Feather!" Her crest went full up, but the officers handling Boyd didn't react to her. They simply marched him through the door to his side of the table. One from the first pair redirected toward the constable, and St. Augustina recognized Detective Rhodes.

Judging from his face, he recognized her too, and it was not an affectionate remembering.

"You have an hour," he grumbled at her, his eyes giving her many warnings and promises if she argued with his pronouncements.

She wasn't the least bit intimidated, at least not in the way he meant. There was too much at stake to win a pointless posturing contest. She nodded, giving him a polite smile. Satisfied, though still not happy, he backed up and crossed his arms.

"That won't be necessary," St. Augustina said, indicating the gag that still bound Boyd's face, swiping her fingers to the right as if that gesture could simply make the gag disappear. The officers escorting the prisoner all looked at each other, silently debating.

"It's her funeral," Detective Rhodes snapped at the reluctant officers.

Then one of the officers dropped a small ring of keys on her end of the table.

"Do whatever you want," she grumbled with a voice made to sell bourbon. "You have one hour. Constable." With a gesture from Detective Rhodes, the escort filed out. A glance at the window/mirror showed St. Augustina the two observing bodies exiting as well.

The courtesy from St. Dominic surprised her. She didn't trust it for a second.

"Thank you," she said to Detective Rhodes. He chewed air for a moment, and she thought he meant to say something more. Instead, he glared back at Boyd. "She was twenty-three years old," he growled. "And we know for a *fact* that it was him that killed her."

"I'm not a judge or a jury, Detective," St. Augustina said carefully.

"No, but you're... you're..."

His dark face grew darker as he struggled to find the right words. They never showed up, and he summarily exited before too many wrong ones tumbled out of his mouth.

She had some sympathy for Detective Rhodes. In other circumstances, she would even admire him; he clearly cared a lot about the victim, but telling him that wouldn't be received in the way she meant it.

Once the door shut, she picked up the keys and crossed to Boyd, who stared at her with wide eyes, or at least as wide as they could go with the cuts and bruises at each temple. She could hear his breathing rasping. She picked out the smallest key from the bunch and gestured to the lock at the side of his head.

Boyd didn't shift at first, staring at her with pure black eyes, as if they could drill through her skull to scoop out her thoughts and motivations for being there. He didn't seem happy about it, but he also wasn't entirely dismissive. Apprehensive was probably the closest word those black eyes could convey.

She indicated at his lock again, a bit more insistently.

At last, he turned his head, giving her permission to come closer. She quickly inserted the key and undid the gag. It came away easily revealing the extent of the damage to Boyd's face.

Officer Papaqui cursed again, in a hiss-y language St. Augustina didn't readily understand. "What did they do to you, Boyd?"

"What do you think they did to me?" he muttered, not at all glad to see his former co-worker or her new boss.

"I see they haven't been treating you very well," St. Augustina said as she dropped the gag onto the table but pocketed the lock with the keys.

Boyd had a coughing fit, then turned his head to spit before rubbing his still-bound hands against his lips. St. Augustina let him get resettled as she crossed back around the table to take the opposite seat, removing the half-bottles of water she carried in her pockets. There were three in total, and she had Boyd's full attention on them by the time she fished the third one out. She cracked its lid and set it down within reach of his grasp. He didn't wait long enough to be suspicious, seizing the water to down the whole mess in pause-less gulps, crushing the thin plastic when it was empty.

"Feel better?" St. Augustina asked, folding her hands on the table before her.

"What the fuck are you doing here, Papaqui?" Boyd snapped at her officer, completely ignoring the Saint.

She heard Officer Papaqui squeak, jumping at the question. "We-We came to help you," she stuttered out, the cool, collected, aloof officer completely gone. St. Augustina knitted her eyebrows at that.

Boyd glared at the coatl, who cowed away, pressing her back against the wall like a dog afraid it was about to be beaten.

"*Officer* Papaqui," St. Augustina interrupted the exchange. "What did you say your relationship with Mr. Boyd here was again?" While her question was to her officer, St. Augustina's eyes drilled into Boyd's.

He flicked his gaze to St. Augustina, "You told her we were partners?"

"I... I... It is in our files, mas—"

"You idiot. Don't—!" Boyd snapped, but he didn't finish his sentence as his eyes darted worriedly to St. Augustina, but it was already too late. She had already seen the interaction and even a non-Saint would be able to interpret what was going on here. Especially as Papaqui flinched away as if afraid of being hit, her crest blazing as high as it would go, even flaring her side feathers out in an involuntary bid to make herself look bigger.

There was more to this relationship than she had originally suspected.

"Mr. Boyd," St. Augustina barked, her voice taking on a cold iron of authority as she stood and leaned her considerable height over the table at the prisoner. "You will address *me* and me alone for the duration of this interview. Is that clear?"

The space between Boyd's eyebrows quirked together, and this time he cowed a tiny bit. A drill sergeant would have tipped their hat at this moment.

When she didn't get a clear ascension or descension, she said to Officer Papaqui without breaking eye contact with

Boyd, "Officer Papaqui, please run out to the car and get me my notebook. I seem to have left it behind."

"Yes, ma'am," Officer Papaqui said, her voice small but steady. She left, taking her winter gear with her, presumably to dress outside of the interrogation room. That suited St. Augustina just fine. Once they were truly alone, St. Augustina settled back on her heels as she reached into her inner coat pocket to remove the envelope of papers that Morlock had nudged her to prepare for this meeting.

"As a designated official of the Magic Guild, I am here to inform you that we will be making every effort to have your custody remanded to us," St. Augustina said formally.

Boyd's eyes narrowed though it was hard to tell between the dark shade of his skin and the dark orbs of his eyes. Then they widened with hope. "Y—" He paused, furrowing his eyebrows incredulously. "*You're* here to help me?" He leaned forward then. "You can get me off? Tiffany, she—"

St. Augustina held up a hand. "I have to inform you that anything you say can and will be used against you in a court of law. You are still under investigation for the murder of Tiffany Williams. The matter of protecting your rights is a wholly separate issue from that."

His mouth hung open for a second, then snapped shut, and St. Augustina wished with every fiber she could have let him keep going since he seemed so ready to talk. Or at least spin her some kind of lie that she could use to start unraveling the truth. She wanted to ask him about the talismans she had found and the hidden case files. She wanted to see him react.

But doing so would only hand this case over to St. Dominic. Not only that but also anything either of them said would only make an easy conviction that much easier. That was not her ultimate goal here today. There was so much more at stake. "I would suggest that if you wish to make a formal statement, you do so with your lawyer present. I can have them come in, and we can get that done."

Boyd sniffed. "As if I would believe for one moment that you're actually on our side." His lip curled. "You talk about jurisdiction, but it's all the same, isn't it? Whether it's under their jurisdiction or yours, it's all the same."

Boyd shifted back in his seat, at least as far back as his chains would go. The blackness of his eyes finally dilated, showing a ring of white around them, which in a lot of ways made them more disconcerting. "Then I want Tyler Morlock as my attorney."

St. Augustina's eyebrow twitched. Well, that was easy. "Of course, you do." She cleared her throat. "Do you have his number? Have you called him yet?"

"I'll get it," Boyd snarled.

The constable shifted into her pocket and fished out the card Morlock had given her. She slid it across the table to Boyd. "Call him today."

"They are refusing my phone privileges," Boyd admitted, his shoulders deflating a little.

St. Augustina narrowed her eyes at that, then twitched her fingers to mark a note in her visual recording to come back to that statement later.

"Alright, I'll take care of it." St. Augustina stood and went to the door.

She didn't even check to see if it was locked; it mostly definitely was. She knocked against its metal surface. After a moment, the door clicked then cracked open, and Detective Rhodes stood there.

"I would like to request a phone for Mr. Boyd to use to contact his lawyer," she said politely but in that firm "it's not really a request" way that promised consequences if not done now.

The man's frown lines deepened in something more of consternated surprise than outrage. He nodded curtly once and shut the door. St. Augustina waited by the door, glancing back at Boyd, but he wasn't looking at her. Instead, he stared down at his hands, looking exhausted and battered.

"Have you received any medical attention since you arrived?"

He glanced up then. "This didn't happen during my arrest," he sneered.

St. Augustina thinned her lips. If Boyd had done half of what she suspected, she wouldn't shed any tears really, but violating the rights of one meant it was so very easy to violate the rights of everyone. And if no one had collected data on such things, she'd need to do something about it.

Detective Rhodes returned and held out a chunky mobile phone out to St. Augustina. "This will log all calls going in and going out," he stated, implying the warning that there would be a record.

"What about privacy?" St. Augustina asked.

"No calls will be recorded, only logged," the detective stated tersely.

St. Augustina didn't believe that for a second. "Thank you," she said anyway with a nod. The detective left and the constable delivered the phone to Boyd. She sat back in her chair while he made the call.

While he dialed, she heard a knocking at the door. She started to stand up when the knocking repeated, but it wasn't coming from the door. The knock repeated a third time, a gentle tapping sound of metal on wood, and she realized she recognized the sound.

Settling back into her seat, she crossed her legs and initiated her communication program. A new icon appeared beside her, forming into an old-fashioned landline telephone sitting on a little single-legged table atop a white doily. To her mind, it appeared as real; anyone else not in her mind wouldn't be able to see it at all as it only existed in her augmented reality. She double-tapped two fingers in the phone's direction, though they only felt air and the receiver rose off of the cradle and floated to her ear.

"Hello, St. Dominic, what do you want?"

CHAPTER 15

<*You didn't answer my knock?*> St. Dominic said, sounding faux offended, his voice hollow as if through an actual telephone line.

<*I've already seen your ugly face once in the last twenty-four hours. I don't need to see it again. What do you want?*> St. Augustina said, or rather thought, since she was only talking in her mind in the Saint's technical equivalent to magic's telepathy tricks. To Boyd on the outside of her, she was sitting quietly with her mouth in a neutral expression.

<*Well fine, we don't have to do this civilly then. Sorry to bother you.*>

There was a long silence. Though St. Augustina was pretty sure he hadn't hung up on her, she decided this was already taking too much time and relented. <*Alright fine.*> The phone floated back to its cradle and she "pressed" a button on the dial face with a small door icon instead of a star or hatch mark.

A door appeared in place of the phone, a wood one with a brass knocker in the middle and brass handle for a knob. It

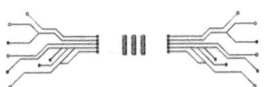

opened, and St. Dominic stepped through ... or appeared to step through. He was a projection into her mind, tricking her synapses into believing they "saw" him. The same was happening to him on the other side. It was a trick only Saints could pull off. He was dressed much as he had been the night before, minus the long winter trench coat. Just a gray suit and a clean shave.

<Beats meeting up in a rundown diner or coffee shop, doesn't it?> St. Dominic asked, smiling that warm Mr. Roger's smile.

<Thank you for letting me access Boyd,> she stated, instead of responding to his question.

<You would have found a way,> he shrugged. *<This way we can talk, and I don't have to waste time fixing whatever you end up breaking in the process.>*

<Are your people alright?> she asked as a courtesy.

Again, he shrugged. *<They're fine. Is the bird woman one of yours then?>*

<You saw her?> St. Augustina asked.

<Yes, of course,> he answered. *<I saw her when you came in.>*

<She came with the job,> St. Augustina confirmed.

<She's very ... colorful,> he noted.

<Behave.>

<What? I am behaving. No cameras or recording devices or anything. Just mind-to-mind. This is top-shelf treatment. Don't get your panties in a twist.>

St. Augustina glanced over at Boyd. He was on the phone, holding it up to his ear, which forced him to spiral his whole body sideways since the chain didn't allow him to hold the phone normally. It forced his gaze away from them. He seemed to be waiting.

"Are you on hold?" she asked him out loud.

Boyd's eyes tried to shift to St. Augustina, or at least, she saw the whites move, but that was all the effort he put in. "Yes," he said tersely.

<Are you doing something to prevent him from contacting his lawyer?> St. Augustina asked St. Dominic, shifting back to nonverbal mind-to-mind communication.

<No. Though I can arrange it if you want more time to talk?> he offered.

<You are the one who wants to talk, St. Dominic. I want my prisoner,> she countered.

<Alright then.> St. Dominic appeared to be leaning against the side of the table, folding his arms and presenting a golden boy appeal that did nothing for her. She wasn't sure why he was even trying but it was like asking why did St. Benedict ever try to be charming or St. Livinus try to be funny. They all had their things. *<What I really want to ask you is: How did you do it?>*

The weight of the question unfolded into a long pause. *<Are you seriously going to make me ask "Did what?">* she asked. Her mind raced to the myriad of things he could be speaking about, but one surfaced at the top, making her skin prickle and her stomach do a belly-flop.

His grin quirked. *<This is just a friendly question. I ran a check. Just out of curiosity. If I understand things correctly, it looks like you were on loan to the Federal Investigation Bureau then, from them to Kodiak Corp. and then you were reported dead for half a minute and then you show up as a constable of the Magic Guild. Everything else in between those bullet points is shrouded in tantalizing mystery, but I can't believe for a second that the Saint program would sell you to the Magic Guild or let you leave to do so without activating your Saint Box and to protect their proprietary property so... This leads to my question: how are you doing it?*

He leaned forward then, examining her neck. *<I see you still have it.>*

St. Augustina shifted before she could control herself, pulling the collar of her coat forward to hide the chain from his view. Though it was tucked under her shirt, his eyes stared hard where it should be, as if he could see it. She felt the false

Saint Box pressing against the sternum of her chest like a lodestone.

He shook his head with child-like wonder. *<How are you tricking the system? Because I cannot for the life of me figure it out.>*

She sniffed. *<And you think I would tell you?>*

He met her gaze with deadly seriousness. *<You don't get what you don't ask for,>* he countered.

<You're not going to get what you do *ask for,>* St. Augustina said, switching her crossed legs. *<My contract is none of your business, and we are not* friends, *St. Dominic. I wouldn't just tell you such a thing.>*

<So there is *a contract?>* he pressed. *<Because when I requested information from the Deacons about the situation...>* He stopped, working his lips as if afraid to reveal too much to her, and knowing he already had. *<They don't usually deny me my requests.>*

She felt the muscles in her jaw tighten despite the rest of her face staying neutral. She was not the greatest at this part, this chess game of faces. Many other Saints were much better than her at reading faces and body language, deriving meaning from the slightest twitch and tick. Strategy, planning, and brute force muscle had been her wheelhouse, so she left this level of espionage training to others. But this wasn't that sort of battle.

How much of what St. Dominic showed her was truth or a well-acted part, she couldn't exactly say, and that was the point after all.

<Something is going on, isn't it? Something big?> St. Dominic leaned in even more. Her synapses reported his breath drifting warmly over her face, even though he was not there. If he tried to kiss her, she would feel it, and if he went to hit her it would report stinging, though there would be no real damage. It was a very vulnerable thing to let someone into your mind ... for both of them.

<Are we done with your personal questions, and can we get to talking about the issue at hand?>

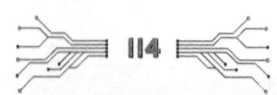

St. Dominic jerked back, realizing he had gotten too close. Despite herself, St. Augustina felt she had just witnessed a genuine vulnerability, now re-masked as he shrugged noncommittally. *<I don't know, is your client finished with his phone call?>*

<You're not listening in?>

<Like I said, that would be rude. And since you're not giving me access to your eyes, all I see is you.>

She eyed his posture, leaning against the table. *<And what, you just happen to be in a room similarly laid out?>*

<It's weird, isn't it?> He stood up to look at the table. *<How the program self-corrects to make us look like we're not being freaky weird to each other. This is actually my desk, but I bet you see the interrogation table, right?>*

<And I suppose I look like I'm sitting in front of your desk in a conveniently placed chair?> She waited to see if he would confirm it and give her some idea of where he was, but he only grinned, so she waved a dismissive hand. *<You were always more interested in this sort of thing than I was.>*

<Because it is fascinating, and you should appreciate it more. We are advanced beings in this crazy, backward world,> he said as he turned to look at something over his shoulder. He made a gesture with a hand and mouthed something just out of her sight.

She scoffed. *<You really do have a god complex, don't you?>*

<And you don't?>

Before she could answer, he jerked, looking up and over her head at something she couldn't see. Just as he couldn't see through her eyes, she couldn't hear through his ears.

<You got to go?> she asked.

He concentrated a moment more, doing a nearly impossible trick of speaking with his real voice while not projecting those same words through his mental connection. Finally, he responded to her, *<Yeah, which is frustrating. I had more I wanted to ask you.>*

<Yeah, I know. I had more I wasn't going to tell you.>

<Well, good luck. I'm still going to beat you over the little vampire because those are my orders. I can only imagine what yours might be since the Cardinals are obviously running a long game, but good luck all the same,> he said straightening up. Then he seemed to slide across the ground and out the AR door, which shut on its own before disappearing.

The second he was gone; she initiated a self-scan on her augs to make sure all traces of him went with him. She would have to run another, more thorough one when she was out of the precinct. Better safe than sorry.

"Constable? *Constable*?"

She blinked and refocused on Boyd, who had finished his phone call when she had been preoccupied with St. Dominic. "Did you reach him?" she asked, as if nothing happened.

Boyd flashed her an uncertain look. "Yeah, he says he'll represent me."

"Good. Until you talk to him, say nothing if you can manage it."

He looked offended at her assertion. "I can manage it."

St. Augustina gestured to her own face, indicating where his was damaged.

He rubbed his thumb against a crust of blood at his temple, as red and normal as an average person's. It would be hard to believe he was a vampire if it wasn't for the blackness of his eyes. "Vampires never have an easy time of it," he said bitterly.

"That's what your aunt said," St. Augustina acknowledged him.

He jerked, and she noted the reaction. A shade of guilt washed his face. "You spoke to her?" he accused, at once looking like a hopeful little boy and a pissy teenager.

"Yes. She's fine. At least as fine as can be expected."

Boyd hooded his eyes, looking like he was about to fall asleep, but St. Augustina recognized it as a defensive reaction.

"Even if you get me out of here, my life is over," he muttered. "Fucking bitch."

St. Augustina's skin twitched at the coldness in the breathy, muttered insult. She knew it wasn't for her, and she didn't get the feeling it was for his aunt. She wanted to ask so badly. She wanted to know if he was referring to Tiffany, and she wanted to follow up that question with many more. But this wasn't the place, and this wasn't the time.

"Boyd. *Boyd*," she repeated, to catch his attention. Slowly the dead eyes looked up at her just under those lids: pools of abyss. It sent a shiver down her spine, but she was a professional, goddammit. She focused on the memory of Boyd's aunt, Morlock, and countless other vampires she imagined cowering in his apartment building. They didn't deserve Boyd's fate. She would make sure that he didn't take them down with him. "I am going to do whatever I can to get you back in our custody. You need to hold on until then. Don't do anything stupid. Don't say anything except when you are talking to your lawyer, and you do whatever he tells you. I *will* be in touch."

With that she stood up and pulled the lock and keys out of her pocket, gesturing at the mask. "Now do you want me to help you put this back on, or would you rather they did it?"

CHAPTER 16

"You want to get something to eat?" Officer Papaqui asked as they walked over the frozen sidewalks toward the Magic Guild Headquarters. The officer stopped and jerked a thickly gloved thumb at a bar front on one of the side streets leading from the train stop they had just gotten off from. "This is where the Magic Guild Guard would go after work if you want to check it out?"

Despite the issues weighing on her mind, St. Augustina had to acknowledge that she was very hungry. And the whole way back from Paladin's precinct, she had been going over and over what had happened with no clear answers.

Officer Papaqui had been a liability. Her interactions with Boyd had been unprofessional at best and downright... syco-phantic at worst. While the coatl had been helpful up to that point, St. Augustina could also see all the long-term challenges Officer Papaqui brought with her.

"You know, that's okay. It's fine ... if you don't want to..."

St. Augustina flinched, realizing she had waited too long to answer Officer Papaqui's offer of dinner.

"No, yes. That sounds like a good idea," the constable said, side-stepping so she could pull open the door of the grill and bar. "After you."

Inside was fairly filled up with people by a weekday's standard. The occupants were as diverse as you would see anywhere in Chicago: everything from business class to worker class made up of every race. Cat People, dryads, hominals, etc.

There were tables with bucket chairs everywhere with a "seat yourself" sign near the front and a three-sided bar in the middle.

Officer Papaqui took the sign at its word and led them to a table in the middle of the room. From that vantage point, St. Augustina could see a small rise in the corner, about five inches off the ground. Just enough to indicate the world's smallest stage. There were no bands there now, but a pair of screens framed a tiny amp with a microphone resting and waiting on top. A pair of office people were flipping through a book near the setup, and it seemed to be filled with laminate pages.

"It must be karaoke afternoon," Officer Papaqui said, still halfway through divulging her winter gear, which she loaded onto one of the two other empty chairs. "We can go somewhere else if you—"

"No this is fine. We're already here," St. Augustina said, laying her own coat over the fourth chair. She plucked up the menu to find it had a QR code in the corner. She scanned that with her ocular implant, and a full list of everything the bar had available appeared in her vision, floating a few feet away as if laid out on the surface of the table itself.

"Just for the record: you're doing a great job," Officer Papaqui suddenly said, finally taking her seat.

"Thank you," St. Augustina said simply and debated with herself between a steak and something called salmon fritters.

"No, I mean it." Officer Papaqui's hand touched St. Augustina's forearm, her scaled fingers ice-cold despite having worn her gloves the entire time. She withdrew them as soon as she touched them. "I just... I get it you know. I wasn't accepted by the other guards either when I first started. I mean, they had to accept me because, you know, I was the token snake person, but it wasn't exactly something they *wanted* to do. Like I said, it was my duty. But you... I mean the way you just kept on after everyone walked out on you. It was ... inspirational."

That was a compliment salad, St. Augustina thought.

"It wasn't like I had a lot of other choices myself, Officer Papaqui," she actually said.

"You can just call me Papaqui, or just Quay. I mean, we're technically off-duty now, right?"

"Quay?"

"It's better than 'Papa.'"

"Yeah, sure," St. Augustina said stiffly, which only extended into an awkward pause between them.

Papaqui's crest drooped. "Sorry. Sorry. Is that being too informal?"

St. Augustina growled in her throat. "No, no, it isn't. I am sorry. You are only being friendly. I just, don't make friends, I'm sorry."

"Oh, I see," Papaqui said. Her crest did not perk up. "Actually. I know what you mean. I'm not the greatest at making friends either."

Before St. Augustina could respond, a large being that looked like he'd been formed out of a square slab of flesh wobbled up to the side of the table, followed by a slight, androgynous waiter with pale green skin, twiddling with their apron between their fingers.

"So, you are the constable we've all heard so much about," the slab said, crossing his arms across his chest.

"Is there a problem?" St. Augustina asked evenly.

"No, I just needed to come over and see it with my own eyes," he stated, sparing a glance at Papaqui. "I understand that you are working to help Boyd."

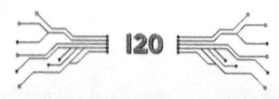

St. Augustina glanced at what she assumed was a Dryad standing next to the Slab Man, only to become aware that the room was listening. "I am."

A tension pooled out of the room at her response. Slab Man thrust a hand out to St. Augustina. "Good. We need one of you on our side for once. I understand you also protected his aunt. Good woman."

As St. Augustina took the hand to shake, she realized what must have happened. "Word travels fast," she said softly. "You know Ms. Boyd." She raised an eyebrow to give it the flavor of a question.

"Word travels fast," he confirmed softly. "Standing up for us takes guts. Your meal is on the house tonight," he declared then turned away to sidestep his way back through the tables. The room started chattering again, and the dryad replaced him to take their order. As soon as she left, another pair of beings took up the space, eager to speak to St. Augustina about a problem they were having with their neighbor. And so it went the rest of the night.

Even their waitress, when she came to offer dessert leaned in. "I just want you to know that I have a cousin who married a vampire. He was killed by police two years ago after claiming he killed an old hominal man down the street. Turned out they had the wrong person. We tried to sue the city for wrongful death, but it's never gone anywhere in the courts and ... and those police officers are still out there on duty. They didn't even try to take him alive. I'm... I'm just tired. I'm tired of people who have done nothing wrong always getting hurt. So thank you, thank you for standing up for us and helping set Boyd free." Green tears poured out of the dryad's eyes; it was all St. Augustina could do to hold it together as she smiled, nodded, and shook the waitress's hand until she went away to collect herself.

The constable didn't get a breath until they finally left.

"Wow, that was amazing!" Officer Papaqui marveled as she flipped through the pages of her officer's notebook, which she had taken out at some point to write down the information from the various complaints. "I can't believe how well you handled all those people. We're going to need a full staff to do just half of this."

"Yeah, it's a ... challenging problem," St. Augustina said, unable to participate in her enthusiasm. "There's another issue I have to deal with first..." She licked her lips in the cold, immediately regretting it as the chapped surface protested. "I want to first thank you for all your help the last few days, but I think it's become very clear that we can't continue to work together."

Her officer stopped in her tracks. "I'm sorry, what?"

"I can't have you in the office ... on my team ... anymore. It was a mistake to have you onboard in the first place." St. Augustina kept her face neutral, even as she braced for a reaction. Taking her to dinner and discussing this then would have been a better tactic, but the goodwill of the magical community had undermined that too effectively. Now she would have to do this the bad way and weather the reaction. She was betting on outrage.

Instead, Papaqui turned to her and lifted her goggles, revealing her serpentine/avian-like eyes. "What is the cause of termination?" she asked very formally, her voice level and eerily steady.

"You think I haven't noticed? That I've been oblivious this whole time?" St. Augustina challenged, annoyed with the question. "I'm not an idiot." She started walking again toward the Guild office, and Papaqui followed.

"I don't understand," Papaqui said, her hood pulsing up as her crest tried and failed to escape.

"Boyd sent you, didn't he? The first day, when you came back."

"What?"

"This isn't amateur hour," St. Augustina spat. "It's clear that there is something more between you two than partners or former work colleagues. I allowed you to stay because I knew I could handle anything you'd do to sabotage—"

"I'm not..." Papaqui interrupted, but she couldn't finish her statement.

St. Augustina met her gaze. "I let this farce of yours run too long before confronting you about it. I kept waiting for you to make a mistake and give me a better idea of what your real objective was, but things are reaching a point where you could jeopardize the investigation."

"But I haven't been! I swear! I... I came of my own volition. I just wanted to help."

"Have you been telling everyone that we are working to get Boyd off?" St. Augustina asked.

Her whole body flinched. "Oh... I... I was talking to the other Guard; you know because they've wanted updates on Boyd and ... I... I think I'm really starting to turn them around about you because of all this. Montgomery asked again about coming back and Running Deer—"

"Then I still have to let you go," St. Augustina said, licking her lips in the cold. "I can't have you in the office or on my team."

"But I just—"

"That's not how I work. That's not the policy of *my* Magic Guild Guard. We do not talk about current and ongoing cases with anybody not involved."

I'm saying too much, St. Augustina kept thinking as she spoke. Honestly, the Saint was aware that she didn't have to explain anything of her reasoning for dismissing Papaqui. In other circumstances, she wouldn't have even explained. She was a little surprised at herself for saying that much.

Under her breath, Papaqui muttered something.

"Excuse me?" St. Augustina challenged.

"You are not objective either," she repeated, her coatl accent thickening as she became angrier. "You've already decided he *is* guilty, haven't you? You're looking at all of this from a corporate perspective."

"I am being objective—"

"Bullshit, you think he's *guilty*, don't you?"

The question threw St. Augustina for a second.

Papaqui's jaw stiffened even more, and then she unhinged it with a frightening pop, extending her face beyond the normal length of most humanoids before popping it back in again. It took St. Augustina a moment to realize it hadn't been a threat or anything, just another unthinking tick from the coatl's alien body language as she proceeded to pop it in and out twice more.

"Please, stop doing that!" St. Augustina finally had to say.

The coatl double blinked at her, then she popped her jaw back in the final time. Her tongue flicked out a second then. "Am I wrong?"

"Boyd murdered—" St. Augustina stopped, closing her eyes for a second as she heard herself doing exactly what she had just accused her subordinate of doing, drawing a conclusion. "The evidence points to Boyd being responsible for this crime. We have no other suspects and no other clues that indicate that something else happened."

"Yeah, but have you been *looking* for any, or are you stopping when you find exactly what you are looking for?" Papaqui sniffed against the cold, before rubbing her mittened hands against her exposed face. Her scales looked oddly pale. "It's never that simple when magic is involved. That's why these crimes need to come to the Magic Guild *Constable's* office. And... And I think we both know that the only reason you're making such headway with this community... No, this consortium of communities is because I didn't *walk out* on you!"

Now, it was St. Augustina's turn to stiffen her jaw.

Dammit.

Papaqui was right.

St. Augustina had just seen it.

Time and time again, when people approached the table to introduce themselves, it was to Papaqui they had gone to first, then the Saint. Should she fire her one and only officer now? How would that look to the community who she desperately wanted to trust her?

CHAPTER 16

St. Augustina looked up at the Magic Guild building where their walking had taken them to as they had talked.

Just then, a chiming cut through the air, like crystals colliding. Papaqui stopped in her tracks and pulled something out of her pocket. Ensconced in the palm of her overly large mitten was a small crystal ball. Not only was it the source of the sound, but it also pulsed with colors like someone had trapped an aurora borealis within. Papaqui brushed her other mitten over the crystal and said something in her coatl language as she brushed that same mitten over where her ear hole would be.

"You have reached the Magic Guild Guard. How can I direct your call?" she said rotely.

A feeling of unease washed over St. Augustina. Something was very wrong.

Papaqui's eyes went as wide as they could possibly go. "We'll be there instantly. We're coming, we're coming!" and she swiped her hand the opposite way over the crystal.

"Someone is attacking Ms. Boyd's building," Papaqui said.

"I have to go!" St. Augustina stated, already whirling in place as she tried to figure out how she would get there without her own car and no idea where the nearest transfer doors were.

"It's alright. I got it. Just hold on to me!" Papaqui said, making another gesture over the orb before offering her other hand.

"What?" St. Augustina recoiled from her.

"Yes, I know you just fired me, but I took one of the emergency relocator orbs from the supply closet. It will take us there instantly. Just hold my hand!"

She had no choice but to accept it.

And then they blinked out of existence.

CHAPTER 17

Of all the magic, it felt like rushing through a wind tunnel for an intense three seconds, and then they stood outside a building on a cold, wintery street. For being so late at night, the area was flooded by headlights. Shouts and screams echoed, followed by a crash of glass. Spinning in place, St. Augustina noted more light coming from all the windows, but her augmented sight reported back billows of smoke from one of the broken windows on the first floor as well.

"There!" St. Augustina barked, pointing at a group of a dozen figures, shouting at the door. Light overlays popped up over them feeding her analyzed data. Several were armed with rifles slung over their shoulders, and most wore Kevlar vests. A couple even had Kevlar chokers designed to repel bites to the neck. All of them wore dark clothes and masks over their faces. Two of them stepped up with Molotov cocktails and threw them through the lowest story window.

"Burn you monsters!" one of the men bellowed with a laugh, pumping his rifle over his head so hard it should have been a pitchfork.

A pair of men stormed out of the building, shouting. One of them rushed the bellowing man, who brought his rifle down in time to block being tackled by the presumed vampire. The two figures wrestled with the gun as another roared and lined up his own rifle with his shoulder, attempting to aim it at the vampire's head. At the doorway, a woman screamed.

"Stop!" St. Augustina barked, her voice projecting loudly off the buildings.

Several of the covered heads flipped toward her as well as a few more ends of rifles.

"This is Magic Guild Guard! You are all under arrest!" St. Augustina roared with her most authoritative voice as if she were backed up by a whole squadron. At that moment, off in the distance, sirens echoed.

"Let's get out of here!" one of the men shouted, and over half the group bolted.

St. Augustina knew she couldn't catch them all; she couldn't even corral them without help. Instead, she pushed forward. Crossing the snow, she grabbed for the two men wrestling for the rifle. Moving faster than most, her arrival startled the masked man. He bucked back, the change of direction upsetting the vampire's balance. The vampire ended up in the snow, while St. Augustina took over the contest for the gun.

"You are under arrest!" she shouted at him.

"Run for it!" his remaining compatriot shouted.

That broke the attacker's resolve. He turned to bolt. St. Augustina moved to intercept him.

"Constable!" Papaqui screeched.

St. Augustina turned back only to see the building going up in flames. Black smoke billowed from the window the Molotov cocktails were thrown through. She just stood there staring. It was like her entire body had locked up. This had

never happened to her before. She always knew what to do, what action to take, but...

She could see the building burning. Could hear the perpetrators getting away. Then she sensed a body pushing past her. Papaqui tore the coat from her serpent-like body, her crest flaring to full-colored glory. Then she ran through the smoke-billowing building's front door.

"Papaqui," St. Augustina whispered. Then the fire alarm in the building finally went off. Or at least it tried, with the bell clanging, then stuttering to clang. Like the invocation of a spell, the sound snapped her out of the trance. "Get out... Get everybody out!"

"My mother!" the vampire she had helped shouted, scrambling up from the ground to run into the building.

Just as he went back inside, Papaqui reappeared, a woman's arm slung over her shoulder as she led a line of three children in tow out the door. The woman had a handkerchief to her mouth and was clearly struggling to breathe.

"What are you doing? Go catch them! I got this!" Papaqui shouted.

A squad car appeared, stopping in the middle of the street. Two officers rushed out.

"You, this way!" St. Augustina shouted. "The perpetrators went that way." She gestured.

"Stay back, ma'am," one shouted as the other rushed up to Papaqui to help take the woman. Two fire trucks materialized on the street, firefighters swarming out of them before they had even come to a full stop. A pack of four teenagers emerged from the building with their arms linked up, carrying an elderly woman to safety.

Tearing herself away, St. Augustina ran. Her enhanced joints moved smoothly. The stabilizers kept her feet from slipping on the wet snow. Her sight enhanced the tracks the criminals had left behind. The tracks led between two of the apartment buildings, barely wide enough for a person to move through. Her augmented eyes highlighted blood streaks on one wall.

They had not gotten far. Two cars drove off, tearing down the icy street, making headway despite the spin on their tires on the black ice. Another truck was struggling, the tires spinning uselessly on the pavement. On her periphery, the license plate numbers popped out, her internal augmentation using her eyes to pick them out even if her attention wasn't focused there.

Two of the men were still running toward a fourth car a short distance ahead of the truck on the one-way street. Both had torn off their masks, and she could see their faces clearly. One of them scrambled for his keys, which he dropped into the snow. The other man hissed at him, tugging on the handle of the car as if that would get it to open. Then he looked up in the direction of their crime just in time to see St. Augustina run up on him. She checked him with her shoulder, her superior strength slamming him into the side of the car. His body dented it, and the perpetrator went woozy, his head lolling drunkenly. A second later, he dropped into the snow.

"Oh God!" his companion cried, terrified. "Oh God, oh God, oh God, oh God."

"Drop the weapon right now!" St. Augustina ordered, wishing she had one of her own in that moment. The one she had knocked against the car didn't seem to have one she could confiscate. Hopefully, the authority in her voice would be enough.

Reminded of it, he lifted the rifle, but his hands shook too much to get it up against his shoulder. Instead, he kept backing away, repeating his chant over and over, but no higher powers were coming for the likes of him.

The man with the shotgun continued to back up into the street, while St. Augustina stayed on the other side of the car, using it as partial cover.

"There is nowhere to go," she said, leveling him with her eyes, which she knew glowed with their blue and yellow light.

"I've got recordings of all of you, of everything you did. Even your friends' license plates. You're all going to be arrested for your crimes, but if you put the weapon down now and put your hands on your head, it can make all the difference for you."

Tears were streaming down the assailant's face in the headlights of the truck. It was clear to St. Augustina that he just wanted out of this situation. The gun even lowered a whole inch as he started to change his mind.

Then the truck hit him.

The horrible bang of his body hitting the front felt like a shot through St. Augustina's own heart. The truck didn't get any farther, skidding and crashing into the cars on either side like a billiard ball hitting the sides of the table.

St. Augustina moved faster than she had ever moved before. Her augmentations had recorded where the man's body had gone, and she went right there to him, lying between two cars.

There was no pulse.

There was no breath.

She started CPR.

She shouted for help.

Help came and took over. She backed away from the body. Other police were arresting the men in the truck and paramedics were seeing to the one she had crushed against the car. She stumbled back the way she came, getting herself together.

"Are you the constable?" a voice asked, a uniformed police officer.

She nodded.

"Detective Rhodes would like to see you," they informed her and gestured to where the gumshoe-like detective stood, speaking to a small group of people wrapped in blankets. St. Augustina recognized Ms. Boyd.

"They sprayed something all over the wall," Ms. Boyd said, gesturing to the side of the building.

"But you don't know if it's the same group?" Detective Rhodes asked.

She shook her head.

CHAPTER 17

"No one saw it happen, but how can it not be related? Are you simply going to ignore—"

"No one is ignoring anything, ma'am. I'm just trying to get the facts, and we'll put it all together. I promise you; nothing is going to be overlooked."

"Why are you here anyway? Where is the constable? You should call the constable. We're supposed to be under her jurisdiction. I know what our rights are!"

"We're looking for her now, ma'am, please..."

"I'm here," St. Augustina cut in. All the vampires turned to her with the same look of relief washing over their faces. One of the smaller vampire children even grabbed for her leg to hug her hard before Ms. Boyd pulled her away.

"There you are," Detective Rhodes said, visibly relieved.

"I was in pursuit," St. Augustina said.

"You caught them?" Ms. Boyd pressed.

"Four of them have been apprehended. We have the license plates of the rest," she confirmed, knowing the information would give them all some relief. "I need to speak to Detective Rhodes for a moment."

Ms. Boyd nodded then asked, "Can we go back into the buildings now?"

"Not just yet," Detective Rhodes said, gesturing toward the building that was still smoking. A crowd of people had gathered along the sidewalks on all sides to watch, but the firemen were walking, not running.

Just then, a CTA bus pulled up on the street and parked behind the firetruck. The detective gestured toward it. "Please, if you'll all go onto the bus to keep warm, the fire chief will let you know when it's safe to go back into the building."

The vampires didn't move until St. Augustina gave them a nod.

Once they were out of earshot, the Saint took charge of the conversation. "What is the situation at this time?"

Not missing a beat, Detective Rhodes gestured to the building. "The fire was contained on the first floor. Only one

apartment seems to be damaged. The fast-thinking grandma was able to put out most of it with a fire extinguisher." He paused a moment, pursing his lips. "Look, before we get into this any further, we need to clarify jurisdiction."

"We were first on the scene; therefore—"

"No, I know. Your officer already gave me an earful. Technically yes, you were first on the scene, and this is also technically a Magic Guild district."

"My officer?" St. Augustina repeated, now scanning the area for the coatl. She saw no sight of her anywhere.

"Yes, yes, she's been all over the place, making sure the victims got medical attention and called that vampire lawyer to come, telling everyone not to talk to us until he arrives. I'll give you credit, she's just as tough as you and knows her city ordinances."

"Thank you. I'll let her know," St. Augustina said neutrally.

"Look, I'm not trying to … show you disrespect, or anything. This is just practicality." Detective Rhodes took a step closer so he could drop his voice quieter.

"We both know you don't have the resources to handle a situation like this. Not only that but also we have jurisdiction over a related case," he stressed softly.

She couldn't argue with his logic. If she had been in his place, she would make the same arguments.

"I agree," she said even as she didn't meet his eyes.

"Excellent, you can—"

"I transfer over the jurisdiction of my crime scene as the constable of the Magic Guild Guard to the Paladin Police Department."

Detective Rhodes' face went still. He understood what she had just done. She had just passed him the case as someone who *had the authority to do so*, establishing her legitimacy as a law enforcement entity. It would have been one thing if she had simply yielded to his authority, but this...

"I'll have an officer come over with the transfer documents," Detective Rhodes said with a curt nod, then he turned to walk away.

St. Augustina scanned the scene again, looking for Papaqui. The fire marshal must have given the go-ahead to the majority of the residents to go back into their apartments because the immediate area and the bus had both been emptied out. Through the window of the bus, however, she saw the familiar back of Morlock, talking to the few people still seated within. Lacking other choices, she headed that way to make an appearance, only to be immediately intercepted by a Paladin officer bearing a clipboard with the jurisdiction transfer paperwork.

She felt an acute sense of satisfaction as she wrote, "Magic Guild Guard," over the line "entity initially on the scene." And there it was. The first legal document that cited the Guard's authority. It was a small victory, but a victory nonetheless. As she passed the completed form on the clipboard back over to the officer, a flag pinged in her augmented vision.

"Papaqui," it said, and it highlighted an outline of a figure crouched beside the far left side of the building.

"Thank you," she said to the officer in dismissal, who didn't say anything in return, and St. Augustina headed directly over to where Papaqui was, hunched down against the wall.

Is she crying? St. Augustina thought. She stopped a few steps away, awkward and unsure of what she needed to say. *Look, Papaqui. I appreciate everything you have done for me, and if you need a recommendation, I'll give you a good one.* Even inside her own head, that didn't sound right. But it didn't invalidate any of the issues she had brought up earlier.

Yet... I think Papaqui's right... But before she could finish that thought, Papaqui collapsed sideways, curling up even tighter into a ball.

"Oh Hell!" the Saint barked, realizing too late that something more was wrong. She hurried forward and tipped her ...

former subordinate toward herself. To her surprise, Papaqui turned into one solid unit like she had already frozen into a ball.

"Too... cold..." she squeaked out, the only sign to St. Augustina that she was alive.

"Help. I need help over here!" St. Augustina called.

"No! Pick her up," another voice cut in coming up beside her to seize Papaqui's other arm. "Her body's shutting down. It's too cold for her."

"We need to get her to the ambulance."

"No, don't bother. She'll be fine, we just have to get her warm. My house is this way."

St. Augustina barely got a glimpse of Morlock before they both lifted the coatl up. Her body was so contracted that she felt heavier than she probably should have been. With her augmentations, St. Augustina could have still carried her by herself, but with Morlock's help, they navigated her down the street.

CHAPTER 18

"**P**ut her on my couch; I have an electric blanket here somewhere," Morlock said, stumbling through the front door. St. Augustina took over carrying Papaqui, heading straight for a black leather couch against the far wall of a fairly small living room.

Where Morlock's office had been an overwhelming mess, his house was a study in fastidiousness. A couch, a chair beneath a bay window, a flat-screen TV with a game system, a large painting over the couch, and one fern made up the room.

Once she got Papaqui to the couch, she pulled a soft gray blanket off the back to cover her with.

"That won't be enough, Constable. She doesn't have her own internal heat source," Morlock called, tearing linens from a closet in the short hallway nearby. "I'm sorry. I'm not finding it. I'll be right back. Try to hold her ... get her body temperature up."

"We should call emergency services," St. Augustina insisted.

"It's just cold shock. She'll be fine once we get her temperature up. Trust me, the last thing you want is to take her to a hospital. They'll just warm her up, charge her a fortune, and send her home again. It's just like the falling iguanas in Florida." Then she heard his feet tromp down some stairs into what she assumed was his basement.

Looking down at Papaqui, she just couldn't imagine that the coatl wasn't dead. Papaqui's eyes were slit open and staring at nothing. Her crest hung limply. Her body was still locked into a rigid ball, and she did not appear to be breathing. All her augmented sight reported back to her about signs of life was that the data was inconclusive.

Quickly, St. Augustina pulled out her phone, holding down the button for voice activation. "Search for everything about falling iguanas," she said, as she shed her coat and gloves.

"Searching, one moment," the phone replied, and St. Augustina rubbed her hands together to make them quickly warmer. Then she placed them against Papaqui's cheeks. Even though her hands didn't feel very warm to her, Papaqui was ice cold.

"Oh, come on, wake up. Papaqui," she said, gently patting those cheeks. It felt strange to slip her fingers over the coatl woman's scaly skin. Then she stripped off her gloves to rub her cold hands. "Dammit, what am I doing? I can do better than this."

Raising her internal body temperature was not something she had to consciously do. The majority of the time her augmentations monitored her internal core temperature and manipulated her chemistry to find her the ideal. As she pulled back Papaqui's blanket, she adjusted her so St. Augustina could slide in behind. Coat open, she pulled the ball of coatl against herself, then reapplied the blanket. In her vision, she engaged her internal systems with eye commands.

"Warning: Raising internal temperature past the threshold will put the subject in danger of a fever," her augmentations warned. She overrode it without a second thought, then settled in to hold Papaqui and hopefully bring her back to life.

"If only we could get this coat off," she muttered out loud, but there was no way to do that with Papaqui's arms locked so tight.

"I'm so sorry. I thought I knew where this damn blanket was," Morlock said, coming back, running a hand through his naturally thick hair.

"It's fine; I figured something out," St. Augustina said as she continued to rub at Papaqui's hands, trying to get the fingers to relax.

"Okay. I'm going to... I guess I'll go put some tea on or something. Just keep talking to her. And be prepared that if she wakes up, she might startle hard and attack without thinking. Just be ready."

St. Augustina nodded. Morlock dropped his coat onto a chair in his dining room and disappeared into the house again, presumably this time to his kitchen.

All she could do was sit and wait. Already she felt sweaty, wanting more than anything to take off her coat and kick off the blanket. Or even go back outside and jump in the remains of a snowbank. Instead, she hugged Papaqui close. Before she realized it, the coatl seemed to slowly melt into her, her limbs going more pliable, the muscles relaxing incrementally.

"There, there. That's it. That's it," St. Augustina soothed, as she worked her fingers through to pull down the zipper on the bubble coat, so the heat could get in faster. It took slow painstaking work, but she managed it, then hugged her closer under the blanket.

"Come on, Papaqui, talk to me. Give me some evidence you're alive."

All at once, the coatl jerked and spasmed, gasping in sharp breaths. Her taloned hands scrabbled at anything and everything around her, which was mostly the Saint herself.

"Papap— Papaqui!" St. Augustina struggled against her, seizing the wild animal on her lap as she fought and screeched, her body spasming as it forced itself back to the living. The coatl fastened herself onto the Saint's body, gripping on with an almost crushing intensity, her muscles locking again there, but this time she was breathing ragged pants.

It hurt, but pain didn't deter the Saint from her purpose. "I got you. You're safe," she said, her vision blinded by the feathered crest standing straight up. "Just breathe. You'll warm up soon."

They stayed that way for a while longer, just breathing and holding. St. Augustina slowly worked her grip around Papaqui, rubbing slowly, distributing the heat through her hands, willing it through the Guard uniform the coatl still wore.

Papaqui's weight became heavier, sinking into St. Augustina's lap. Then all at once, the talons retracted. St. Augustina gasped at the sudden relief in her shoulders, upper arm, and upper back. Her charge tensed again at the sound but didn't reinsert the talons. Instead, she simply clung and even nuzzled against her at one point, the source of warmth bringing her back to herself.

"You're going to be alright," St. Augustina just kept repeating so much that the words had started to lose their meaning.

"What..." Papaqui croaked out.

"You got too cold," St. Augustina said, latching on to the question.

"Hmmm," she moaned, sounding both painful and regretful.

"Morlock helped me get you somewhere warmer," the Saint continued. "You... You did a good job. You helped a lot of people. You helped me."

Admitting it aloud shook St. Augustina as she realized she was going to do something she had never done for someone who had ever worked for her before: she was going to give her a second chance. She immediately went into questioning that decision, picking at the flaws and doubts so much that she hadn't realized she had stopped talking.

"l ... am ... sor—" Papaqui tried to say, but she shuddered again, then added. "l let you ... d-d-d—"

"No one got hurt. And there was no way l would have gotten to them in time if you hadn't known what to do," St. Augustina said, both to herself and her... her officer.

Officers don't hug together for warmth, St. Augustina internally chided herself, followed by, *Oh no, we are not going down that train of thought.*

"Look, Papaqui, it might be a Hollywood cliché, but l got reason to not trust people. l probably got more reason now than ever before being what l am for a bunch of people who are all magic, but ... l did trust you ... and today ... that might be why l took your unprofessionalism with Boyd so hard. l—"

"You were right. Boyd did send me." Papaqui forced herself up to a more sitting position but didn't have the warmth to go very far. She clung the blanket to herself, hanging her head so her crest fell forward. "The night we all quit, at the bar... we all thought he was joking at first, but he had been serious. He told me to go back and keep an eye on you, report it back to him, and l don't even know why l listened to him. l just did, you know? He's got a way about him that you just want to do what he says. So you are right; you should fire me."

Papaqui trembled as she moved to get off St. Augustina's lap, but the Saint put a hand on her shoulder, and the cold-blooded person leaned into the warmth.

"Not yet. You're not warm enough yet."

She nodded mutely and leaned back, letting St. Augustina pull her close again. Her body wanted to melt against her warmth, she could tell.

"What have you told him?" St. Augustina asked.

"Nothing. The first time l've seen him since was at the station."

"What is the relationship between the two of you?"

Papaqui flinched again. "l... l can't talk about it," she admitted, "l'm sorry, l just can't."

St. Augustina's nostrils flared, her mind racing to the reasons that would be true. "You and Boyd were more than just partners then? At least at one time."

"I can't talk about it," the coatl repeated. "Please don't ask me."

"I'm not asking you to. I understand," St. Augustina said, her mind going to all the things she herself can't say to others about the people who had controlled her life for so long. Now she wanted to put Boyd away for good more than ever.

"I want to stay," Papaqui said, this time the words clearer if still soft. "I see what you're trying to do and what kind of Guard office you want to run, and I want to be a part of it. I'll do better. I promise, but please let me stay. I have nothing else in my life, and I know I can do better."

"I'll do better too," St. Augustina agreed just as softly. While they had talked, Papaqui's body had uncoiled itself, her skin becoming soft and pliable again. Again, the coatl sat up, looking at St. Augustina with hope. Though they were close together and this felt like an intimate moment, St. Augustina got flashes of snuggling on the couch with her little brother. Or rather, Papaqui seemed like the little sister she had always wanted.

A whistle pierced the air, which immediately died.

"Do you think you can sit up and drink something?" St. Augustina asked, shifting her weight to encourage the idea. She had lost circulation in her legs and really, really wanted to stop sweating.

"Uh, yeah. Yeah, thank you," Papaqui said, and complied with the shift to slide onto the couch itself, the blanket still wrapped around herself.

"You look a lot better," Morlock said as he returned, bearing three mugs with paper tags on strings coming out of them.

"I'm so sorry about this," Papaqui said, taking the one he offered her. "It was so hot inside, I threw off my coat, but it was so cold outside when I brought people out. I struggled to manage the speed of the temperature shifts. Did everyone...?"

"Yes, you got everyone out. Other than some smoke inhalation, no one was seriously hurt," Morlock said, handing St. Augustina the other tea while he himself sat down in his armchair. It was only because of her extra-long arms that she managed to reach it. "I would say that you've done much to help your reputation with the magical community today."

"I'm just doing my job," St. Augustina said.

"But ... shouldn't you still be out there processing the crime scene?" Papaqui asked, blowing on her tea to cool it down.

"I passed jurisdiction over to Paladin," the constable said, getting the reaction she expected from the statement.

"That's not good," Morlock noted, while Papaqui gasped.

"We don't have the resources to hold on to those we caught," St. Augustina replied. "Not yet anyway."

"At least tell me you signed it over officially?" the vampire lawyer moaned.

"Yes, I did."

His head jerked up at that. "Oh. Well, okay then."

"So that means, you got them to officially recognize the Magic Guild Guard as a legitimate department?" Papaqui asked, putting it together.

The Saint nodded once. "Yes. Considering the situation, it is a small tic in the win column."

"I will be representing the injured parties in the case, pro bono, unfortunately, but it is considered part of my tithe back to my community, so that will at least get my mom off my back," Morlock grumbled, then sighed. "And I suppose you're right. The Magic Guild Guard does not have the resources to deal with this and handle Boyd's case. This was a pretty big deal. I'll try to help people understand that."

"Thank you," St. Augustina said. "I should get my officer home."

The term was not lost on Papaqui, whose crest rose up along with her eyebrow ridges. "Um, yeah. We still have work tomorrow. In the office."

"Yes, of course," Morlock said.

"And I can take myself home... if you can just call me a cab, I'll be fine, really," Papaqui insisted. And continued to insist until they relented. The battery for the internal heating coils within her coat had died, so Morlock loaned her all of his hot water bottles to provide a heat source within her coat. St. Augustina felt better about the whole thing when the cab driver turned out to be another cold-blooded person, and the heat was cranked to Sahara levels. Between Morlock and her, she managed to get into the car just fine, and St. Augustina tipped the driver extra to make sure she got into her apartment.

Once Papaqui was gone she shook Morlock's hand and turned away herself to go to the nearest Opener Shop, when she was stopped halfway down the block.

"Ms. Boyd, I'm glad you are alright after all the events of the evening," St. Augustina said politely, but the vampiress waved her polite words away.

"I must see you tomorrow. I have information for you about your case," she said abruptly.

"I see," St. Augustina acknowledged, "if you like, I can find a quiet place, and we can talk now."

"No, no," Ms. Boyd said with a wave, "it is important, but I cannot talk now. I must take care of Coletta's kids, and they are not going to sleep much tonight. I have too much urgent things to take care of, but I will come to the Guild office tomorrow and we will talk."

"Oh, I see. I understand. Well, that would work for me. I had some more questions I wished to ask you," St. Augustina noted.

"And there we are," the older woman said, and then she turned with a wave and marched back down the street.

The urge to follow, to try to do more to help, washed through St. Augustina, but she knew it would not be welcome really. If she wanted to help, she needed to keep to her role and keep manipulating the strings in the hope of unbinding these people from the trap they found themselves in, not of their own making.

CHAPTER 18

"Get some sleep, St. Augustina," she muttered to herself as she walked down the street to the main thoroughfare. "Can't help anyone if you're exhausted."

CHAPTER 19

I n the warm light of the office, Ms. Boyd looked much as she had the night before in a light blue sweatshirt this time proclaiming the vampire knitting circle of 1995. Her face was also more haggard.

"Here's your coffee, ma'am," Officer Papaqui said gently, setting the cup down in front of her on St. Augustina's desk. Despite the lack of extra ears in the Guild Guard office, St. Augustina thought it made more sense to meet in her office space with a shut door. Ms. Boyd smiled weakly up at the coatl, who nodded with her version of a gentle smile.

"Thank you, Papaqui. You are always a dear," she said, before wrapping her hands around the plain ceramic.

"You know each other then?" St. Augustina asked from her place on the other side of the desk.

"Yes," Ms. Boyd answered before Papaqui could. "She is Boyd's partner."

"Is? Not was?" St. Augustina raised an eyebrow. Papaqui's crest skittered, clearly aware of the thin ice she was skating

on. She had just earned her job back, and they couldn't count on another murderous mob to save her again.

"Oh, actually, I don't know if that is true anymore." Ms. Boyd looked back at Officer Papaqui for confirmation. "I know you were all doing a partner switch system for a while there."

The officer nodded vigorously, which looked a bit funny as she still had her coat on with the hood up over her head, presumably to keep warm. "Yes, we switched a while ago." Papaqui retreated back, visibly uncomfortable with the inquiry.

I can't hold this against her, but no need to let her know that just yet, St. Augustina thought wickedly, maybe enjoying Papaqui's nervous energy a little too much. *I'm going to turn out exactly like St. Benedict if I'm not careful.*

"Ms. Boyd, you told me last night you had some more information for me Is it about the talismans we found in the apartment?" St. Augustina pulled the evidence bag from inside a drawer to lay them out before Ms. Boyd on the desk. She had gotten to the office with exactly enough time to retrieve them from the evidence book and set them on her desk.

Ms. Boyd's eyes turned black at the sight of them. "Yes. I know what they are," she said tightly.

"Farmecul pentru a lega strigoii," St. Augustina said, repeating word for word what Morlock had already told her.

Ms. Boyd froze a moment, surprised to hear the term before she could say it. "In general, that is more or less correct, but I know specifically what kind of farmecul it is."

"That I do not know," St. Augustina acknowledge. "Or specifically what it does and why these ingredients."

Ms. Boyd took a long drink from her coffee as if the brew could fortify her. Then she made a sign in the air before her face, ending with her kissing her thumb, before directing that thumb toward the objects. "These are a bastardized version of an old, old vampire magic. This is not the magic of Obayifo, but of Lamia. During World War Two, many vampires relocated to the United States from Eastern Europe, attempting to escape the fighting. Many more returned, volunteering for the

US Army forces to prove their loyalty to the new country. The mothers intended to protect their children. It was their wish."

Ms. Boyd seemed to be implying something that the Saint just couldn't read. "I don't understand," St. Augustina said.

"What I am saying is, it did not start as something malicious. Having children is a difficult process for us; they are few and far between. Vampire mothers would give their lives to save their children. And many of them did." Ms. Boyd bent down to her purse and pulled out an old book with an ugly tan cover favored in the 70s. It was already bookmarked with several tabs, but she selected the third most one to open the book with before passing it to St. Augustina.

The text was written in vampiric runes, her implant already working to translate it, but the picture captured her attention. It looked like a reprint of a wood carving. A squat figure holding something like one of the talismans in one of its hands.

Ms. Boyd indicated St. Augustina to turn the page. On the other side were a pair of black and white pictures of a washed-out woman, possibly in her late middle ages, just short of elderly. Her head was covered in a tied scarf. At first glance, St. Augustina would have said she was dead, except no corpse she knew of sat up like that without supports. In the second photograph stood a somber-looking scientist, complete with a white coat and the especially round glasses popular in the 1940s. He was obviously posing for the picture with a hand on the woman's shoulder. The caption underneath was also in vampiric runes, but the listed names of Dr. Albescu and Mrs. Albescu were easily discernible in the text.

She looked up at Ms. Boyd for clarification of what she suspected she was being shown. The learned vampiress nodded. "They turned themselves into false vampires, demonic thralls bound in service to their sons who returned whole from the war after miraculous recoveries."

"Why would their sons do such a thing?" St. Augustina asked, wrinkling her nose.

"They did not. The mothers did it. They misunderstood the charm and knew only that giving their children such things could bring them back alive. But what it did was draw on their life sources, transferring it to their sons' no matter how far away they were, until nothing was left of their life forces. By the time what was happening was understood, it was too late to help them."

"Goddess," Officer Papaqui exclaimed, laying a hand against her stomach, then she began trembling.

"Officer Papaqui, are you alright?" St. Augustina asked as the coatl's crest noticeably shook.

"I... no..." She held out her hands so she could see them shaking. Her crest rose in alarm. "Oh, no." She gestured to her crest. "This means... This is what we do when we feel sick. It's not fear. Not afraid. But I think I might throw—"

"Okay, okay, I understand," St. Augustina nearly shouted, and she waved her hand to stop Papaqui from continuing to explain. Instead, she refocused on what Ms. Boyd seemed to be telling her. "So, you believe that Boyd read or learned about this charm thing and duplicated it."

Ms. Boyd nodded. "Yes. Yes, he was always a good magic study, which was why we were all surprised when he joined the Guard. It can be a very dangerous job, and I think he may have made these charms to try to recreate the protective effects. It is all forbidden, illegal magic."

"Then I think I need to ask why you even have this book if this sort of magic is so dangerous?" St. Augustina raised an eyebrow.

The older woman blinked. "This book does *not* contain the spell, only the history of it. The consequences of it. I do not know where Boyd would have found the actual spell," she said defensively, and St. Augustina supposed that was a fair reaction.

The Saint gestured with a finger to make a note in her implant recording as a question to follow up with Boyd at a later date if she got the chance. Carefully, she closed the book. "Does anyone else know about this?"

Now Ms. Boyd shook her head vigorously. "Not likely. I spoke only to Morlock. He contacted me when he took on my nephew's case. I am a Lamia and keeper of our people's lore. His questions sent me on the correct path to finding this. I have been searching for answers since we discovered it in Gerald's apartment, but I was looking in the wrong places. This volume was in my own library. It is a mostly forgotten part of our history."

Immediately, St. Augustina thought of the other Saint involved. "Could anyone other than you get this information independently?"

This time Ms. Boyd bit her lower lip, the point of one of her fangs pressing against the red of her flesh. "That I cannot say one way or another."

"Yes, that was what I feared." St. Augustina nodded. "And I suppose there is no cure."

Ms. Boyd shook her head. "No. Once you are dead, you are dead. Despite what pop culture would have the world believe, we do not truly return from the dead, ever. Believe me, this truth still haunts the oldest of us. The men who returned were horrified to discover what they had done to their mothers. How many near death experiences that resulted in miracles were only because they had consumed the life force of their own mothers to survive. I am counseling two such vampires now. Old men who have had to live with what happened and are only now talking about it. One is suffering from dementia, his memories..." A guarded look shifted over her face. "It is a tragedy."

St. Augustina nodded sympathetically. "I can only imagine." She closed the book and tapped the top with her index finger. "May I keep this a while."

The Daughter of Lamia nodded. "Until your case is resolved, you may keep it in trust as a sign of good faith from our community."

"You have nothing to prove to me," St. Augustina said carefully.

"We all have much to prove to each other," Ms. Boyd said.

The Saint nodded then held up the book again. "So you think that Boyd created something similar, possibly more than once, based on these talismans, in order to draw on the life force of his victims to keep himself alive?"

"It is my fear, yes," Ms. Boyd nodded. "He has had many close calls during his service. The false vampires created this way, they would be in service to him, and they would need blood to survive."

St. Augustina's eyes went wide. "The blood kit. Officer Papaqui, did we get a copy of the results of the blood kit? Was it confirmed to be Boyd?"

"No, ma'am," Papaqui said, still looking ill.

"Morlock has received it," the vampiress said. "He called me. The blood kit shows that it was not Gerald who bit Tiffany."

"Then that proves that Boyd didn't kill her!" Papaqui cried out, too excited.

"Or his weapon was his false vampire. You said he is in control of the false vampire."

"Yes, complete control as long as it is fed blood regularly and can hear its master's voice."

St. Augustina sighed. "Okay, last question: do you happen to know who could be Boyd's possible false vampire?"

Ms. Boyd shook her head. "I am sorry but also not sorry, Constable."

"I understand and thank you for this. It has been extremely helpful." Everyone stood up, and Papaqui escorted her out while St. Augustina continued to stare down at the talismans on her desk. When her officer came back, she asked, "Have you heard back from the lab yet?"

Officer Papaqui shook her head, making her crest dance. "No one is returning my calls."

"Alright, fine," the Saint said, picking them each up, then opening a drawer beside her to pull out the small map wall book she had been studying. "If tech isn't going to help us, time to see what we can get done with magic."

CHAPTER 20

"I think we have both come to the conclusion that Boyd didn't kill Tiffany," St. Augustina stated as she gestured her holoboard into existence. The wall of light shone in the middle of the Guard office space, hovering over two of the desks that they had shoved back to make room to work.

"Yes," Papaqui agreed, as she finally found a working pen to take notes with having gone through three already.

St. Augustina gestured and Boyd's picture from his Guard file as well as Tiffany's from her driver's license appeared on the board with the titles of suspect and victim respectively. "We know that Tiffany was bitten. Even though we don't have her coronary report, we can tentatively conclude at this point that she died from being attacked."

She wrote to the side the words "motive?" "We don't know what the motive would be to attack her."

Then she wrote with her finger between them "bite kit-negative" between the two images. "We just know it wasn't Boyd who bit her."

She listed the talismans to the other side of Boyd. "But someone, likely Boyd, but it could be Tiffany since she lived in the same apartment, used these talismans intended to make a false vampire."

"You think Tiffany did this and got eaten by her own creation?" Papaqui asked, her crest sticking straight up.

"No, I don't think it's likely since if it had been Tiffany, Boyd would be telling everyone that to prove his innocence. But it is possible she found out about the false vampires. Maybe she confronted him about it. Maybe she just found out about the talismans themselves and recognized that they were used to make false vampires?" St. Augustina kept turning the various puzzle pieces over in her head, trying to see if she could get any of them to fit together.

Her officer looked down at the talismans, now spread out on one of the vacant desks. "Are we sure that's what the talisman's are for?" Papaqui asked. "We don't have the actual spell to be sure."

St. Augustina slapped her hand against her forehead. "Oh, I am such an idiot. We should check to see if the Magic Guild has the spell somewhere. Don't they have a restricted magic library?"

"Yes, I already called up there to put in the request," Papaqui said, "The librarian didn't know of anything off hand, but she said she would let us know if she found something."

The Saint smirked. "I think I could get used to this."

"What?"

"Having a subordinate who knows what she's doing."

Papaqui tried to suppress her pleased smile, but it didn't work. "Thank you, Constable."

They lapsed into thinking silences, both looking at their gathered evidence and theories so far.

"What if..." Papaqui started then stopped.

"Yes, officer?" St. Augustina prompted.

"What if those talismans aren't all used? You can make something like that, but have you used it yet? What I mean is,

could whoever made those things still be alive?" She stood up and went to the map wall. "If they're alive, there is a way to get this thing to show us where they are on the map." She looked around but couldn't find what she was looking for until St. Augustina held out the command book with its fingered pages.

"Can you figure out how that works?" the Saint asked.

"Yes, I think I can do that," she said as she looked from the talismans to the map wall. "At least, it's worth a try."

"You said only if they are alive? So this would not help us locate Boyd's false vampire?" St. Augustina pulled a chair over from one of the desks so she could sit and take in the whole wall map. At that moment, it showed her an overview of the city, divided into its major neighborhoods, the whole thing representing 2.7 million people.

"No. The technique I know will only show us the living. Since we have the blood and hair samples here on these talismans, we can use that to find them. It's what we do in missing person cases. Or we did, when we had any." Opening up the worn pages of map wall's book, Papaqui flipped to the back and read something laid out there. Then she started knocking an elaborate rhythm on one of the panels. It took a couple of tries, but eventually she got it to form a blank square just in front of her on which she pressed the first talisman against.

"One ... two ... three ... four ... five," Papaqui counted out, the map swirled around, some blocks staying still, others moving and shifting with lines popping up and dissipating in no discernible pattern. Then the map held still, all a jumble of tiles.

"Okay, I think we can safely assume this person's dead," the officer declared, laid the talisman down on one of the evidence books, and shut it safely inside before going to the next talisman.

St. Augustina said nothing, simply watched the process as Papaqui repeated it, one talisman after another. The map continued to swirl, some of the panels holding still. The chaos of it became mesmerizing until something caught St. Augustina's eyes. Down in the lowest corner, two small panels had formed their own little image with the relief of a take away coffee cup and two small creamer containers beside it. When Papaqui pressed another talisman to the blank square and all the panels would swirl, the coffee cup would wobble and clack, like someone was shaking it.

Coffee. With creamer, she internally puzzled at it. Then above it, another panel appeared, this time showing St. Augustina's badge with its hazelnuts on it. That image kept moving up and down, bouncing on top of the coffee image. Furrowing her eyebrows at it, the hairs on the back of her neck rose, the sensation one felt when they were being … watched.

She turned to look over her shoulder and practically jumped out of her chair when she noticed the grotesque above the door was blatantly staring at her. Looking back at the coffee cup, she went back and forth a couple of times. No matter what Papaqui did, the coffee image stayed the same, shaking most vigorously.

"Hey, Papaqui…" St. Augustina started.

Left, right, left, right went the grotesque's head; its eyes practically blazing at her.

"Yeah?" Papaqui answered, not looking up from her work.

"Do you want some coffee? I was thinking of running down to the shop on the first floor," St. Augustina asked smoothly. The grotesque stopped shaking his head.

"Actually, no. That's okay, I'm not hungry. But you go ahead if you want," she said with the absent-mindedness of the intensely focused.

"I think I will. Moving around helps me think," the Saint said as she evenly got to her feet, not making any sudden moves that would break Papaqui's focus.

She still wore her long, winter coat and decided not to shrug it off as she left the room. The grotesque didn't move its head anymore to follow her movements, its gaze staying fixed on where she had been. Or maybe it was keeping an eye on Papaqui, she wasn't quite sure.

"Yeah, I know, coffee with two creamers," she said to it softly as she passed underneath. "Am I a constable or a gopher?"

Out in the hall, when she stopped to wait for the elevators, she noticed another of the grotesques at the end of the hallway positioned so it could watch whoever came out of the elevators or through the fixed transfer doors. This one was also moving its head, distinctly going from center to over toward the transfer doors. Again, St. Augustina narrowed her eyes at the motion. It stopped when she turned away from the elevators toward the direction it wanted.

The hairs on the back of her neck rose.

There were three doors before her, each with their destinations on plaques above them.

She looked back at the grotesque for a little more guidance, but got nothing from the statue.

"Where are you trying to take me?" she asked, but again, the grotesque didn't move. She looked back at the three doors. "Okay, then how about which one do you want me to go through?"

This time the grotesque blinked, she was sure, like it hadn't expected that question and didn't know what to do. Instead, it shifted its head one more time toward the transfer doors helplessly.

St. Augustina thought about it a second, then pointed to the first door labeled Lincoln Square. The grotesque shook its head no. The next door was labeled "Under Wacker," and the third had a more stylized plaque with two little trolls in profile facing the word "Bakgate." When she pointed at that door the grotesque nodded its head vigorously. Exhaling a breath, she glanced back toward the Guard office doors.

"I guess there was an extra-long line at the coffee shop," she said before stepping through the door.

The hall she emerged into was larger and darker than the one she just left. It took her a minute to adjust and shake off the stabbing pain that threatened a headache, but once she did, she was shocked to see where she was. It wasn't really a hall

CHAPTER 20

but more like a large arced tunnel made of dark, oily-looking bricks. Standing 20 feet tall at the apex, stores with glass windows and hanging wooden signs lined the space for as far as her senses could perceive.

Glancing behind herself, she realized she stood in front of a wall blocking off the end of the tunnel. This was covered with a mural though it was harder to see in the dimmer light of the gas lamps framing it. Someone had painted an archway, which she stood before, and on either side of the archway was the impression of a stonewall relief depicting trolls of various sorts laughing, drinking, singing, and in general being happy. On the ground to either side of the painted arch were two stone statues of trolls, each about St. Augustina's height. They were caricatures of trolls, with round happy bellies and long rounded noses, dressed in clothes that would have been in fashion in Norway during the Middle Ages.

Before St. Augustina could take in anything else, one of these statues turned toward her. She jumped out of her skin, but then it pointed down the tunnel between the shops.

She peered at it warily. "Is that..." but then realized that she had no idea if whatever intelligence was guiding her through the statue had a name or not. "Is that ... you?"

It nodded and pointed again insistently down the tunnel.

"So you have something to show me that has something to do with Boyd's case?"

It nodded again. Then pointed again.

"And you don't want Papaqui to know about it because she was Boyd's partner?"

This time, it didn't nod or shake, but it pointed rapidly down the tunnel as if getting impatient and annoyed by her questions.

"Alright, alright," she placated, holding up her hands, and did as she was bid.

The shops on either side looked interesting enough. Much like Lincoln Square, there were all kinds of shopping to be found here, but she didn't have much time to actually do it.

Unlike Lincoln Square, many were very troll-themed. There were even a few people, mostly trolls, moving up and down the tunnel, in and out of the shops. A troll-themed flower shop, a food stand, a troll antiquity store, etc.

She stopped in front of one that seemed to be a kitsch shop of troll souvenirs for tourists, if the shirt that declared "I went to Bakgate, and all I got was this awesome shirt!" could be believed. A troll was inside the main building of the souvenir extravaganza, leaning on the counter reading a magazine with a bored air while two customers were comparing coffee mugs with different slogans and Nordic-themed pictures.

St. Augustina moved away from the shop, only to be confronted by another statue of a troll, this time painted in bright colors symbolizing a tourist with a perm held back by sunglasses and an old-fashioned camera on a strap around its neck. The Hawaiian shirt it wore was covered with tiny Sears Towers and Chicago-style hot dogs. It was also moving, gesturing back toward the kitschy store vigorously.

The Saint mimicked the gesture. "In there? What you want to show me is in there?" It just kept pointing insistently, only to stop the second the mug-buying tourists exited the store.

Blowing out a breath, St. Augustina shook her head as she went back toward the store. "Oh come on. It's not like this is the weirdest thing you've ever done. You're just following a lead. From a grotesque. At the minimum, I can get coffee mugs for the office." The fact that the grotesque had shown her a coffee cup on the wall map hadn't removed that possibility.

"Let me know if you have any questions?" the troll woman said with a bored tone. She didn't even look up from her magazine as St. Augustina entered.

"Actually, I do have a few questions if you have a moment?" She stopped just in front of the counter, fishing out one of her business cards to present to the clerk.

"Yeah?" the clerk said, straightening up, taking the card with concerned eyebrows.

"I'm Constable St. Augustina with the Magic Guild Guard. I was wondering if I could ask you a few questions about a former officer of the Guard, Gerald Boyd."

The troll clerk's eyes widened a moment, and she dropped the card as if it were on fire. "Oh God, you've come for him. You've finally come for him," she barely whispered.

Okay, maybe this is more than about coffee mugs, St. Augustina thought, as she repositioned her feet. The troll woman was about equal in height to St. Augustina, which was saying something since she was artificially tall and strong. Maybe it was her own prejudices at play there, but the Saint couldn't help it. She didn't say anything, just kept her eyes on the troll woman.

"Please," she whispered, visibly trembling. "Please don't take him away from me."

St. Augustina continued to regard her, her mind racing to what this woman could mean, and not liking any of the options.

At last, her shoulders slumped in defeat. "I knew we should have left the city. It was only a matter of time."

She turned then and threaded her way to the back of the store. St. Augustina followed with her hands in her pockets, prepping the right one for a troll-level shock if needed.

A sense of foreboding skittered through St. Augustina's skin when the shop clerk opened a door that went down below. It smelled wrong. Not just the usual cloying damp of underground spaces. It smelled dead and sour.

"Please. Can't you just look the other way this one time," the troll woman begged, wringing her hands so hard, the Saint thought she'd break them off.

"What is your name?" St. Augustina asked instead.

"Marigold," she replied in a small voice.

"Marigold," the Saint repeated in the same level of voice, but firm where Marigold's was quavering. "Everything is going to be alright."

The troll's eyebrows popped up at that before pursing back to worry. With a shaking finger, she pointed. "He's... down there," she whispered.

Not wanting the troll to get behind her, St. Augustina gestured for her guide to go first. The troll shook her head in refusal, but the Saint insisted. The cheap wood of the stairs creaked and even wobbled as they went down. St. Augustina wasn't able to see anything until she reached the bottom.

So that's what a false vampire looks like, she thought.

CHAPTER 21

"Who the hell are you?" the harsh voice asked through sharpened teeth. Everything about that mouth looked like it had only one purpose, to rip and rend flesh. Like the vampires it was based on, the false vampire had deep, black, soulless eyes that seemed to suck out the light in the room.

He sat at a messy desk amongst several shelves of boxes, labeled with things like novelty mugs, 24-count boxes of kitsch, and a t-shirt press sat on another table behind him. There was a single source of light in the room, a desk lamp that glared a sad yellow beam down on several messy stacks of papers. The vampire himself didn't seem like he had been doing anything amongst the work, just sat back in a bucket office chair wearing, she couldn't believe it, a dark red velvet smoking jacket.

The false vampire seemed to be examining her as much as she studied him, recognition finally crossing his face. "Ah, of course. You. You're finally here."

"Derrick, please. You should get out of here—"

"Shut up, Marigold," he said with a practiced air of matter-of-factness.

Startled, Marigold flinched and crouched back, like a dog afraid of a beating.

"You'll have to forgive my familiar, Constable. I can't seem to train her properly to know her place. She just doesn't listen."

The troll woman gave a tiny mew, which caught his attention again. "Who is minding the shop, Marigold?"

Again, the troll woman flinched, then turned and barreled past St. Augustina, to charge up the steps. St. Augustina stumbled off the last step as she went past, which was awkward, but she was unharmed.

The false vampire chuckled. "You have to admit, what she lacks in brains she makes up for in enthusiasm." He picked up a martini glass from amongst the junk on the desk and took a sip of something thickly red.

"And I have to admit I have been curious about this tin woman the Guild hired to be the shepherd of our little flock. Rumor has it you have motor oil instead of blood. Is that true?"

He cocked his head to one side like a smart-ass teen who believed they were poking at something incredibly funny.

"I don't think I know you well enough to share such details," she said evenly.

"Hmm, pity. We'll just have to get to know each other better then."

"I'll be honest, you weren't what I was expecting either."

He lidded his eyes and managed to look even haughtier. "Oh, really? And what were you expecting, pray tell?"

"If I'm honest, I was expecting to find a mindless drone. I was given to understand that false vampires were nothing more than soulless monsters."

The false vampire slammed his fist on the desk. "Do I look like a soulless monster to you?!" he howled.

If he expected St. Augustina to be intimidated, he was sorely disappointed. She didn't flinch or look away.

He sighed and took another sip of his blood martini in a show of collecting himself. "Apologies. It's been a trying day already. My name is Derrick. But you know that, of course. And as to your other colorful comment, I am not a 'false' anything. I am a vampire, the same as my sun-loving cousins. The only difference between us truly is that they are afforded protections for their compliance when someone like me is persecuted and destroyed on sight. I ask you, do you think that's fair?"

He then leaned over to reach into an already open drawer in the desk and pull out a thick brick of bound-together dollar bills. Printed on the paper wrap around the middle was "$10,000" in red ink. "On the off chance, would this settle things between us?" he asked, holding it up.

St. Augustina smirked at it.

He waited a moment for her to say or do something more, but when she didn't, he tossed it back into the drawer. "No, I suppose it won't, but you can't blame me for trying. So, what is it you do want? I would rather not destroy you if I didn't have to."

She almost laughed at the way he didn't even bother veiling his threats. "It's not about what I want, it's about what the law requires," she said.

"Oh, don't give me that sanctimonious crap. We both know the law is only for other people who fit their molds perfectly and sit up like good little sheep, not for predators like us."

Another testing gambit. He wasn't sweating, but it was the only thing missing from this scenario. Instead, St. Augustina could smell the foulness grow stronger, and it was clearly coming from him.

"Was that part of the deal you had with Boyd?" she asked, playing her own gambit.

"We've had our understandings." Then the false vampire's grin deepened, showing more teeth. "Ah, I see. No, that makes sense. You need to clean up your predecessor's loose ends, or are you looking for the same thing? It is a dangerous job.

Maybe even more so for someone like you." He looked her up and down suggestively, and she had a brief flash of how satisfying it would be to punch his rat-like nose in.

He settled back in his chair, seemingly satisfied that he had found his bargaining chip and had already won the game. "Alright then, I will tell you everything I know about Boyd. I even have the evidence you need to take care of him for good." He then gestured to another chair that was piled with stacks of catalogs and other papers.

Apparently, he expected her to clean it off for herself to sit. Any and every little micro-aggression he could do to try to have every slip of power over her.

"I'll stand," she said flatly, keeping her hands in her pockets and the charge waiting in her fingertips.

"Suit yourself," he said. "Anyway, let's cut to the chase. Boyd did call me the night his false vampire murdered his girlfriend. Paladin police already came by to ask questions, but Marigold managed to deflect them competently enough so they never even spoke to me, which means I'm only giving you this exclusive testimony." He grinned. "Who loves ya, baby?"

It took St. Augustina a moment to realize he was quoting Kojak, and since it had been decades since that detective show had been on TV, she wondered if he realized most people wouldn't get the reference.

"You do, apparently," she said, smirking to herself.

"And don't you forget it. I like doing favors for people. It's just my nature."

"So he called you?" she prompted.

"Yes, wanted to know if there was a way to reverse what he had done, bring his false vampire back to life. Of course, I told him there wasn't because what is dead is dead."

"What did you tell him?"

"That it was his own fault for not keeping a tighter leash on his thrall and his girlfriend and that it wasn't my problem. Then I immediately hung up because I have my own problems. I wouldn't have to be dealing with you or Paladin if he had just had a little bit of consideration for anyone else, you know what I mean?"

"He struck me as very selfish," St. Augustina agreed, just to agree.

"Exactly. All I did is like what I'm doing for you, helping you out so you can help me out. Mutually beneficial." He pulled a key out from around his neck on an overly long chain. He had to lean to fit the small thing into a lock on one of the desk drawers, but it turned easily enough. Inside he pulled out an old book. It had no real spine to speak of. Instead, it seemed to just be a series of uneven pages bound together with leather between two tattered covers. He opened it and turned a few pages before thrusting it out to her. "I believe this is what you are looking for."

She recognized the vampiric runes. "This is the spell Boyd used to create false vampires."

"Yes, he came to me one day begging for some means to save his life. I, of course, was willing to do my part for the Magic Guild Guard, and gave him this solution to his problem."

St. Augustina was sure that the meat of that story was a lie, but she rolled with it. She was sure she would get a different story from Boyd, if he ever cared to confess. "And in exchange, he looked the other way in regards to your existence." She didn't need him to answer that. "How does this work then? I don't read Vampiric."

"It's rather very simple. You choose a suitable host. A little hair and blood to bind it from that target and then as long as you have it on your person, touching your skin, should something unfortunate happen, the damage that would have gone to you is passed to the chosen one."

St. Augustina furrowed her brows. "I would think that would just kill the host. Why does it make a false vampire?"

Derrick shrugged. "I have no idea, but it does. And once the life force is completely drained, then you're left with an obedient servant. They may not even realize they are dead at first, but over time ... well ... all things decay. The hosts will

also develop an insatiable thirst for the life force of others and will try to drink blood to obtain it. That's where one can run into problems. If I'm honest, I've thought about doing it to Marigold, but she's already a pain enough to manage."

"And she's a troll?"

He scoffed. "What does that matter? Life force is life force. She would even be more powerful and strong. True her troll body would have its limitations. Like for example, you enthrall a mermaid. Well, no matter how enthralled they are, they are just not going to be able to function at all on land. Their bodies are not made for it, so you have to be deliberate in who you choose. Pros and cons."

"Powerful undead slaves on one hand, with a maintenance cost on the other," St. Augustina noted.

"Precisely, you have the idea."

"Is there a limit to how many you can make?" she asked, thinking of the six talismans they found.

"No other than it's stupid. You do it enough, you're going to get caught eventually. Having one minion is hard enough to manage."

And yet, St. Augustina could see how a corporation could use such a thing to their advantage. The upper echelons do love their slaves and having the means to protect their lives no matter what? It would be worth the cost of using a Saint, and St. Dominick's interest in this case suddenly became far more clear.

"So you are not one of Boyd's false vampires?"

Derrick was unamused. "No," he hissed. "My creation is none of your business."

"Do you know who is?"

"No. Once I gave him this, I had no idea what he did with it. Nor do I want to know."

"Hmm," she said and scanned her eyes over the page of the book before turning to the next page.

"What's wrong?" Derrick asked, just short of a shout.

"I highly doubt someone of your savvy and intelligence would not keep tabs on someone like Boyd. Especially since you now had an in at the Magic Guild Guard."

"I know when and where to play my pawns," he said.

"I would like you to come down to the Guild office to make a state—"

"No!" Now Derrick stood up, revealing himself to be a much shorter man than herself. "That is not our deal."

"I don't recall agreeing to any deal," she said, shifting her weight to the balls of her feet.

His lip curled up to snarl as he drew the right conclusion.

St. Augustina pulled her hand from her pocket. "Now Derrick. We don't have to do this. We don't have to fight, but you know I can't leave you here like this. You have to come in with me, and we can sort—"

"Go to hell," he spat, then charged with a pointy tooth snarl.

"Well, it was worth a try."

CHAPTER 22

Moving down the hallway of the Magic Guild toward the Guard office, St. Augustina didn't think her limp was that noticeable at all. It hurt like a sonofabitch, and she would probably have bruises all up and down her one side, but all in all things could have gone much, much worse. For one thing, she could have been dead.

It was too bad that electrical shocks didn't work as well on an undead nervous system as they did on everyone else's.

"At least, it slowed him down enough," she muttered, as she paused to lean a hand against the wall and catch her breath. It had actually taken more time to get Marigold to stop freaking out after St. Augustina managed to impale Derrick on a broken chair leg, which sure enough caused him to burst into a pile of dust. So at least there was no body left to explain.

There was no way the situation wasn't going to come back and bite her in the ass, especially after Marigold ran away, but at that moment, St. Augustina decided securing the book was more important. So she had limped her way back to the Magic Guild and hopefully Papaqui's help.

To her relief, she found her officer sitting at one of the desks, studying a talisman in her hands. She didn't look up when St. Augustina came through the door, and the Saint took up residence against the door frame to catch her breath.

"Hey, Papaqui," she called. "I think I have a lead on who Boyd's false vampire may be, but I need you to come help me."

"It's me."

A brief silence followed the abrupt statement.

"What?"

Papaqui stared straight ahead, her gaze so far away she could have been a statue, but at the pressure of the Saint's gaze, her eyes shifted to meet it. "It's me. Oh, Goddess, I'm dead," she breathed out. She held out the talisman toward St. Augustina.

It was like the others, but instead of being a twist of hair, it was broken and roughly shaped feather similar in color to the ones on Papaqui's head.

When St. Augustina didn't move closer to take it, she stood up to walk it over, only for her legs to give out from underneath her.

That spurred St. Augustina from the doorframe. "Papaqui! Papaqui, are you alright?"

The coatl didn't exactly answer, but sat on the ground by the door, her head wavering back and forth, her crest drooping. A molted feather wafted beside her.

"No, no, don't touch me," Papaqui tried to say, pushing away the Saint's hands as she went to help her up. She crawled away a couple of feet then stopped. Lifting up on her knees she stared down at her hands, which visibly shook. More bits of feather fluff floated around Papaqui's form on the floor. "Where is it? Where did it go?" she cried, realizing she had dropped the feather talisman.

St. Augustina picked it up gently. "Papaqui?" she asked just as gently.

The coatl flinched, cupping her hands toward her body, her body heaving with pants.

"What makes you think you are a false vampire?" the Saint asked cautiously, taking another step to the side to begin circling around. "This... This could be anybody's feather."

The coatl leaned forward, rolling herself into the same ball she had when she had been too cold.

"Papaqui, answer me," St. Augustina ordered, then squatted down beside her.

Then with desperate urgency, she got up and moved past the desk she had been working at.

St. Augustina rose to follow, keeping one step back and prepared for anything.

Papaqui yanked open one of the cabinet doors, a breath of frosty air rolling out of it as she stared into it.

To St. Augustina's surprise, the cabinet had several brown bags, two plastic lunch boxes, and the takeout box from Selamarie. They were piled on three shelves and lit by a small crystal glob hovering at the top of the cabinet. A few drinks were also wedged between the bags. And a hodge-podge bunch of condiments sat in a little tub to one side. Nothing about it seemed terribly out of the ordinary other than the cabinet was not what St. Augustina would expect a fridge to look like.

"What am I looking at?" St. Augustina finally asked.

"My lunches," Papaqui said, her voice monotone and heavy.

St. Augustina blinked rapidly, trying to and failing to understand. "Okay?"

"All of them. They are all my lunches. I keep bringing them, but I don't eat them. Boyd... he must have been removing them so I wouldn't notice."

"What?" St. Augustina leaned in and plucked out one of the bags. Sure enough, over the surface was scrawled the name "Officer Papaqui" with black marker. She traded it for another that said the same thing. Every one of the bags, take out trays, and lunch boxes said the same thing, over and over in the same handwriting. "Officer Papaqui, Officer Papaqui."

"1 was looking at them yesterday when 1 dropped off my takeout box from the restaurant," the officer said, gripping the cabinet door so hard it bled color from the scales on the back of her hand. "1... 1 can't remember the last time 1 ate a meal."

Her other hand reached into her crest and pulled. St. Augustina was about to protest, but the feathers came away easily. She held them out to the Saint, who took them despite her urge to pull away. "I've been losing scales and feathers over the past day. It's why I've been keeping my coat on. 1 didn't want you to think 1 was sick and tell me to go home when we had all this important work to do."

St. Augustina looked at the feathers, then to the back of Papaqui's hand, which was indeed peeling scales away. She licked her lips carefully. "So far, all you have shown me can be attributed to signs of severe depression—"

"The thing Boyd have me do to save his life," Papaqui cut her off as she turned away and went to her desk. Her case book was already sitting there, retrieved from the cabinet and she flipped it open to a pre-marked spot in the book. "I've never felt so connected to someone in my life. It's like 1 took the life right out of myself and gave it to him. Everyone says this makes me a hero. Maybe things are going to be different between me and Boyd from now on. This is what partners do. They save each other."

She offered the book to St. Augustina, who took it, scanning over the words.

"1 wrote this in my report. He made me do some sort of ritual to save him when we had that bad altercation. But 1 don't remember it. If it's the one that Ms. Boyd has described, then *I am* the false vampire."

St. Augustina eyed the female before her again, watching her shoulders rise and fall with every desperate breath. "False vampires are dead, Papaqui." She set a hand on her shoulder. "You're breathing. You're thinking. You're not a mindless corpse or some twisted evil thing in a basement."

"What?"

The Saint shook her head. "The point is you're alive!"

Abruptly, Papaqui's shoulders stopped moving. St. Augustina stared down at her hand, then at Papaqui's quiet face.

And they waited.

And waited.

The tension built as St. Augustina's internal clock, wired to be perfect, ticked inside her.

Two minutes.

Then three minutes.

Then five minutes ticked by.

And Papaqui still hadn't taken a breath. She didn't even seem like she needed to.

Slowly, at last, St. Augustina lifted her hand from Papaqui's shoulder and set two of her fingers into the place in the bipedal serpent's neck, feeling for a heartbeat. She couldn't find it, no matter how many times she reset her fingers.

"You can't find it can you?" Papaqui asked.

"Just... Just wait." St. Augustina triple blinked her eyes, and she called up her augmented sight and ordered an assessment before her. Within a few beats of her own heart, she had a list appearing beside Papaqui. Body: Dead, indeterminate number of days. With a list of vitals underneath. Heartbeat, b/p: 0, O_2 levels: 0, etc.

Brain activity: Present.

"I checked with the map. It can't find me." She gestured to the wall, and sure enough, it was showing a view of the office from the grotesque's point of view. It showed the two females in the room, but St. Augustina glowed as a living officer of the Guard. Beside her Papaqui visible but the same color as the rest of the room. "Ma'am, the law is very clear about this. You have to destroy me."

"Papaqui."

"No, it is the *law*. I am a monster... a-a-a-a-a thing now. I'm a walking dead body animated by magic, oh Goddess." Her crest trembled again, then she stiffened her spine, locking her

arms behind her back like a soldier at parade rest. "I'm a danger to everyone around me."

"In the last few days, I have only seen you help people," St. Augustina said.

Papaqui closed her eyes. "I'm pretty sure I killed Tiffany."

"We don't know that is what happened."

"Actually, we do." Both females turned to see Morlock standing in the doorway. He looked disheveled, like he had been in a wrestling match in his business suit and had lost. He held up a folder of papers in his one hand, dropping his coat over the back of a chair with the others. He held out the folder to St. Augustina but never took his wary eyes from Papaqui.

"What's this?" the Saint asked, grasping the folder to flip it open.

"The report of samples taken from the scene of Tiffany's murder. The DNA found in her bite wounds that most likely killed her does not match Boyd," he said gravely.

"We already knew that," St. Augustina snapped at the unwelcome interruption.

"They match me, don't they?" Papaqui asked.

Morlock hesitated, one eye narrowing inquisitively at her. "They know it's a coatl bite."

Papaqui turned toward another supply cabinet, tearing it open to pull out a bite kit, knocking several other things to the ground in her haste. "We need to take a sample immediately!" She tore the package open and thrust the cotton swab into her own mouth.

"Papaqui! Calm down!" St. Augustina ordered.

The coatl thrust the swab out toward the Saint. "Please run it. I know it is a match! I'm the murder weapon!" A strange humming noise came from Papaqui's throat. Alarmed St. Augustina looked to Morlock, who only looked freaked out in return.

She knew snake people didn't shed tears so... "Papaqui, are you crying?" she asked carefully.

Papaqui grabbed at her throat. "I'm sorry. I'm sorry. I'm... I'm trying to be brave." Her crest trembled. "I don't... I didn't want to die."

"No... but you want justice, right?"

"What... What the hell are you saying?" Morlock shook his head, his eyes growing wide.

"This situation is not as straightforward—"

"You can't do this! Don't you understand what this would mean for my people!" the vampire shouted, slapping his hand against his chest. "We're alive and our lives are threatened every day because of the sins committed by these... these flesh puppets!"

"Morlock—"

"She's not real! She's dead! You protect her and you risk the lives of every vampire in the city!"

St. Augustina took a step between him and Papaqui. "It's not your call to make."

"She's right, it's not," the voice of Lady Ursula cut in.

The Guild Guard office door swung shut firmly behind her as the elegant woman and the head of all of the Magic Guild stood there in resplendent orange. It was like the sun had entered the gloomy gray room.

"Now, I think my constable should update me on what has happened?"

CHAPTER 23

apaqui continued to fiddle nervously with her formal uniform, doing and undoing the middlemost button, her talon clicking on the brass surface. St. Augustina wanted to order her to stop it, but it would have done no good. She looked in the mirror in the waiting room, adjusting her own collar when Morlock entered.

"They are almost ready. We'll be called to enter soon," he said, looking nervously from St. Augustina to Papaqui.

"Are you sweating, counselor?" St. Augustina asked, a dry attempt at a joke, but she wasn't reassured when he pulled a flask from inside his front jacket pocket and took a swig.

"The judge is the Honorable Cartwright, so some sweating is understandable," he stated.

"Cartwright? I thought the judge was Alvarez-Hughes?" Papaqui squeaked as she reached up to pluck at her thinner crest, only to have St. Augustina intercept the hand and direct it back down to her side.

"Judge Alvarez-Hughes has a personal relationship with me and so had to recuse himself from the case. We've been assigned Cartwright, which isn't bad exactly; she is a Magic Guild sanctioned judge. She's... Well she's tough. Reminds me of one of my college professors. Doesn't care for shenanigans in her courtroom and definitely wants all sides to prove their argument and not waste her time. What we are about to do would definitely be nothing less than a shenanigan."

Papaqui made a humming noise until St. Augustina set a hand on her arm. "Keep it together," she ordered. When Papaqui nodded, St. Augustina moved to readjust the officer's collar. "I know it's been a hard month, but you have this." She slipped the chain around Papaqui's neck to show her the emblem at the end, the Magic Guild symbol imprinted on a coin the size of a half dollar. "You are an officer of the Magic Guild. You can do this."

Papaqui wrapped her fingers around the coin, squeezing it tight. "Yes, Ma'am," she said quietly but firmly. "Boyd won't be there, correct?"

Morlock looked up from the device he was taping at to answer the question. "No, no. I am his representative in this hearing, but the petition is coming officially from the Magic Guild against Paladin Police Force."

That meant St. Augustina was the representative in charge of making the jurisdictional case against Paladin's representative, St. Dominic. Naturally.

A bell went off internally at the same time Morlock's device chimed. The constable and the attorney looked at each other, opened their mouths to say, "It's time," closed them instead when they noticed the other, and then nodded understanding. It would have been funny if things weren't so serious.

"Is it time?" Papaqui asked, having not had her own alert, but hearing Morlock's go off.

"It's going to be fine," St. Augustina repeated, though she gave a fidgety twist to the new ring on her right-hand finger. Morlock's expression also didn't support that statement.

They filed out of the room and headed into the venue; the guard stationed at the door glancing only at Morlock's pass before waving them all through. The uniforms spoke for themselves apparently.

"How is it a closed hearing if he's not checking everyone at the door," Papaqui whispered, but St. Augustina only set a hand on her upper arm and steered her to their seats near the front.

The venue was the same as most courts. There were the judge's bench and two tables facing it. Both tables were empty of papers or equipment. St. Augustina had no need of anything more than herself and Papaqui. She glanced over at the other table as she positioned herself to stand behind her own.

St. Dominic was there, though he hadn't acknowledged her yet. He was leaning into another person she didn't recognize, speaking softly to them. Detective Rhodes came up, but St. Dominick gestured him away from the table. The hardworking detective stood there a moment, clearly disturbed at his dismissal but St. Dominic didn't acknowledge it. After it was clear there was nothing more the detective could do, he glanced up at St. Augustina. She kept her face neutral, but his twisted in anger anyway, as if this was all her fault somehow.

Maybe it was, who was she to say? If the Magic Guild had not hired a Saint as their constable, would Paladin, and by extension Kodiak, have brought in their own to take his case away?

Whatever the answer would have been, it didn't matter, and Detective Rhodes turned to take his seat in the audience.

At last, St. Dominic turned to her and stood up to cross. She met him halfway, symbolically not allowing him any space in her "territory." He grinned at her as if recognizing what she was doing.

"Well, let the best man win?" he asked. Of course, he would use the word "man." He was as subtle as a tornado.

"Let justice be done," she answered instead.

The other Saint's eyebrows quirked at that. That had always been St. Dominick's major flaw, other than the homicidal tendencies that the Deacons saw as an asset. His expressions and thoughts were impossible for him to hide fully. He was a blunt-force instrument, not a poker player. Unfortunately, that flaw was not something she'd be able to really use to her advantage here. They were playing for the judge, not each other.

He stuck out his hand, and she shook it, which allowed them to break away from the Saintliness-measuring contest.

"What was that about?" Papaqui asked, her crest popping her formal cap up in the back, threatening to fling it off her head entirely.

Before St. Augustina could answer, the door opened. The bailiff called out for all to rise. The minimal attendees to this hearing obeyed as a slight, older woman walked in with a swirl of black robes and took her seat formally behind the judge's desk. Once she sat, everyone else was allowed to follow suit. She lifted up a pair of glasses from a long chain around her neck and set herself up to read from a file.

"Now, I am given to understand that today's hearing is closed, and all records of today's proceedings will be sealed under Magic Law, except for the judgment, is that agreed to and understood by both parties."

"Yes, ma'am," the Saints said in unison. St. Augustina had traded many concessions to get this one in return. It would be worth it.

"Alright then, since this is a hearing and not a trial, let's hear it," she leaned back in her seat, taking her glasses off her face to pin St. Dominic with a steel-colored stare. "Why should the Paladin Police have jurisdiction over a case that clearly falls under the auspices of the Magic Guild Guard."

It had been a toss-up which one she would start with, but St. Augustina conceded their luck that the Magic Guild sanctioned judge was already leaning toward in the direction she had been intended when given the designation. She wished she could just count the case won, but she doubted it would be that easy.

St. Dominic telegraphed, at least to St. Augustina's perception though probably no one else's, consternation at having to go first and be on the defensive, but he stood and gestured with his hands. Light erupted from them as his holodesk appeared, covering the table before him. There was an audible gasp in the room from the few court officers in attendance.

"I would like to present to the court the facts of the case—"

"Wait, wait," the judge declared, waving her hand with the glasses still clutched in them as if it were a baton and she a very annoyed band director. "What is this? Holographic evidence is not permissible in this court."

St. Dominic stopped a breath as if he hadn't expected that, and it was St. Augustina who stood.

"With all due respect, Your Honor, it is in this rare instance when the holographic evidence is submitted by a cybernetically enhanced being known as a Saint." She turned to Morlock who already had the one sheet of paper they had brought held out to her. She took it and turned back to the judge. "Permission to approach the bench?" she asked.

Judge Cartwright pursed her lips into a perfectly straight line, but she gestured and both Saints came up to speak with her. St. Augustina proffered the paper, which the judge took.

"It is not very common that one side comes to the other's defense in these cases," Judge Cartwright stated, looking over the small legal brief she had been handed.

"In this instance, it also helps my own case, as I will be submitting information via hologram today as well, ma'am. A Saint's brain is equipped with a digital augmentation so that the evidence we present in this way is the same as would be presented via any computer. There is already case law concerning this."

"I see," she murmured, and the judge continued to read. At last, she sighed and set the page down. "Very well, I will allow it, especially since you will both be submitting evidence in this

way, but I want to make it very clear to both of you that I do not care for shenanigans and tricks in my courtroom. This is your one and only warning, am I understood?"

"Yes, ma'am," St. Dominic said a second before St. Augustina and she shot him an annoyed look.

"Alright, students, back to class," the judge said in a humor so dry, St. Augustina only smiled on her way back to her side's table when she realized it had been a joke.

"Now, if I may, Your Honor. The case we are dealing with is nothing other than a simple homicide that happens to involve a vampire and nothing more that would relegate it to the Magic Guild auspices." He then proceeded to display the facts of the case of Tiffany Williams via his hologram. He showed pictures of the victim and her alleged murderer, the crime scene, the coroner's report, and the various other forensic reports, including the DNA found in Ms. William's wounds. But he only showed that there was a verification that the wounds were inflicted by a vampire through the presence of vampiric enzymes in the wound.

"...and according to Hermetic Law, in the case of death caused by biting, even if the death was a part of a culturally protected practice within a home, the death itself is not protected and therefore still rises to meet the threshold for wrongful death charges, which the City of Chicago has brought to bear against Mr. Boyd. There is nothing inherently 'magical' about what Mr. Boyd did to Ms. Williams that then resulted in her death."

The judge studied St. Dominic's holographic case board before turning to St. Augustina. "Do you have anything to rebut about the Paladin case at this time?"

"No, ma'am. My counterpart has done an admirable job of laying out the evidence that he has. I do not contest any of it at this time. I do have further evidence that may alter the interpretation of those facts, but that *is* why we are having this hearing."

"So you withhold contest?"

"Yes, ma'am."

"Let the record show then that Magic Guild accepts the evidence presented by Paladin with no contestation at this time."

The stenographer nodded as he made a note.

When he had finished, Judge Cartwright turned to St. Augustina. "The Magic Guild may now state their case as to why they are requesting the onerous task of turning over jurisdiction on a case they are not contesting the facts of, apparently involve no magic, and that the Paladin police have a serviceable track record of closing?"

St. Augustina rose, looking the judge squarely in the eye. This was it.

"Because we have evidence that shows that this case is part of a much larger case involving multiple crimes, we allege that Mr. Boyd is not only responsible for the death of Ms. Williams but also the deaths of six others." She gestured, and her holodesk opened up over her table. It was pre-filled with the case boards for each victim, made small so they could all fit within the confines of her display, but not easily read. It had taken every minute over the last month to track down the remaining five of the six victims and compile their information. Boyd had done a good job of covering his tracks.

The judge leaned forward, her glasses snapping onto her face.

St. Augustina could feel St. Dominic's gaze boring into her, but she didn't dare glance at him. This wasn't over yet.

"We suspect that Mr. Boyd is involved in the wrongful death of Thomas Kaid, Carla Marino, Tiki Chi..." she continued to list each case that they had uncovered. Many of the victims had been transients, people on the street, but two were people he knew, including Papaqui. When she got to the end of the list, there was not a person in the room that was breathing.

Judge Cartwright's eyes continued to roam the screen, eyes picking out details, her face as taciturn as a statue's. "You're going to have to help me out here, Constable. I do not see anything that unifies these deaths."

The moment where they would either win or lose everything.

"They were all killed with the same murder weapon," St. Augustina reported. "There are arguments that several of these would have died anyway of other causes and those causes are what were stated in the initial reports concerning their deaths." St. Augustina gestured, bringing up an image of the tokens they had found in Boyd's apartment. "We were able to locate these in Mr. Boyd's apartment..."

"You removed evidence from a closed crime scene?" St. Dominic challenged, the first thing he had said the whole hearing since his presentation. Now St. Augustina turned to face him as he stood up, his fist clearly pressed into the top of his table.

"I was granted permission to enter by Mr. Boyd's aunt, Ms. Boyd, who is also the holder of the lease. Together we found this evidence inside a magically sealed box that no *hominal* policing force would have been able to discover otherwise." She stressed the term the magical community used for anyone who was purely human.

"Have a seat Paladin Police, you'll have your chance for rebuttal," Judge Cartwright said as firmly as a patient teacher who's been instructing unruly students too many years.

Only his training allowed St. Dominick to obey the authority in the room. His glare told her he had not expected her to come up with such a good counter to his case, but to be fair to him, there had been no other signs that this was in fact a serial murder.

"Proceed, Constable," the judge invited.

St. Augustina enlarged the image of the talismans so it filled the holodesk. "These items are composed of a mix of hair or feathers, herbs, and drops of blood that we have been able to tie to three of the victims."

"Not all?" the judge asked.

"Some of the bodies of these victims already identified were claimed and the remains disposed of according to

their customs. There is a petition in process now to have the bodies exhumed and samples taken to verify the rest," St. Augustina supplied and pulled up the order for the judge to see, then nod at.

"I will require a copy of that order. Continue," the judge gestured. "Is this all you have?"

"No, Your Honor. We have identified the murder weapon and have it in our possession."

"Your Honor!" St. Dominick exclaimed, standing up with an exasperated throwing of his arms. "We already know, and it has been accepted by this court that Tiffany Williams was murdered when her throat was ripped out by Gerald Boyd."

The judge slammed her gavel. "I do not tolerate outbursts or dramatics in my court. Sit down, sir. This is your final warning."

St. Augustina thought she heard the opposition's table crack as St. Dominick griped the edge to aid in retaking his seat.

"Your Honor, I must also apologize. I am about to pull my dramatic act myself, but I hope by the time I finish my explanation it will become clear why."

Judge Cartwright's eyes narrowed. Then she said carefully, in clipped tones, "Your time is yours to do with as you see fit, Constable."

The Saint had to resist the urge to swallow. "You see, Honor, these six are not the only victims of Mr. Boyd. We discovered a seventh victim, his last one. Officer Papaqui of the Magic Guild Guard."

At the sound of her name, Papaqui bolted to standing, clasping her hands behind her back to hide their shaking.

There was a long silence in the venue.

"Carlo, can you please reread for me the last thing Constable St. Augustina said," Judge Cartwright requested.

The stenographer scrolled back on his tiny screen. "You see, Your Honor, these six are not the only victims of Mr. Boyd. We discovered a seventh victim, his last one. Officer Papaqui of the Magic Guild Guard," he repeated, billboarding the coatl's name at the end.

The judge looked from St. Augustina to Papaqui. "Constable, if I am not mistaken, Officer Papaqui is standing alive and well next to you."

St. Augustina nodded. "Officer Papaqui is standing next to me."

Judge Cartwright opened her mouth to say something further but then stopped and narrowed her eyes again. The woman had clearly caught St. Augustina's careful omission. Then she sat forward very slowly as she seemed to understand that omission's implications.

Setting a hand on Papaqui's shoulder, St. Augustina pushed on. "During the course of our investigation, we discovered that Mr. Boyd had been attempting to create a false vampire. The other six victims were his attempts and failures at this. His seventh succeeded, and it was this false vampire who killed Tiffany Williams. He was able to hide this fact in plain sight by ordering his creation to act as she would if she remained alive. And so, she did.

"Officer Papaqui continued to conduct herself as she always had with no one suspecting anything, while she was working to solve this case. Because of this, she is the singular instance I know of, of someone having solved their own murder. Magical legal precedence dictates that in the case of a false vampire being created, any crimes committed by that false vampire are the sole responsibility of the one who created them. An undead being is not a person but a thing."

Papaqui's crest trembled at that last part, but other than that she stood straight and solid under St. Augustina's hand. "This makes Officer Papaqui the murder weapon. Which is also why it is imperative that Mr. Boyd be moved to Magic Guild custody. The magic he used to create this false vampire who can act like a normal person is a forbidden magic that must be dealt with by magical authorities who can deal with and dispose of this knowledge before it falls into the wrong hands—"

The Saint didn't get the rest of it out.

St. Dominick moved fast, charging at her periphery.

St. Augustina barely managed to turn in time.

Time seemed to slow.

The room hadn't reacted yet.

He attempted to dodge down, anticipating her interference.

She anticipated his anticipation. She hooked his leg.

His body turned; he braced to counter.

Fire burned down St. Augustina's arm. Her blood sprayed across the table. The hologram stuttered.

St. Dominick flipped the blade around in his hand as he turned. He exposed his back to bring the blade around to Papaqui's throat.

All this happened so quickly, the coatl was still turning toward the attack.

More blood sprayed.

The knife deflected away.

Papaqui dropped to the ground.

Morlock screamed and grabbed at his arm. He had swung it around Papaqui's neck to grab her and throw her to the ground. The knife scored along the back.

The living vampire clasped his wounded arm against his chest as he howled. Then he vomited straight into St. Dominic's face.

St. Dominic recoiled in horror.

St. Augustina punched at the same time. She connected with the back of his exposed head.

His neck snapped too far to the side. St. Dominick dropped along with the knife. He landed beside Papaqui on the ground.

Morlock's body bucked to heave another arc of vomit.

St. Augustina kicked the knife away toward the courtroom guard.

Then time sped up back to normal speed.

CHAPTER 24

The venue was in chaos. The judge stood up slamming her gavel over and over. The stenographer screamed, backing away from the violence while taking the stenography machine with him. Morlock continued to heave, trying to move away, which just meant that he trailed more vomit after him. St. Augustina thought he had to be empty soon, but then he started to dry heave.

On the floor, St. Dominic lay unconscious in a pool of the attorney's sick. St. Augustina's augmentations reported that he was alive but very unconscious, so she left him where he lay and went to Papaqui.

"Are you okay?" she asked offering her hand to Papaqui still lying on the floor.

The coatl accepted it, letting herself be pulled to her feet. "I think so."

"Hold it, don't move!" Detective Rhodes shouted. He stood flanked by the court officer, the only one allowed a gun in the

room. That gun was now pointed straight at Papaqui. At least, until St. Augustina stepped in-between.

The judge continued to bang her gavel. "I want order right now!"

St. Augustina stared down the gun unflinching. "This is unnecessary," she said, loud enough for the judge to hear.

Two more bangs. "Constable, do you understand you have brought one of the most dangerous of the most dangerous creatures into my courtroom?"

The Saint held up a hand toward the judge, showing her the enslavement master ring on her fourth finger. "I have her contained, Your Honor."

Papaqui held up the amulet around her neck on the end of the chain over St. Augustina's shoulder toward the judge.

"I repeat, she is under Magic Guild control." This time St. Augustina directed the statement to the gun-wielding officer.

A heavy pause held the room. "Stand down," Judge Cartwright ordered.

The officer held his gun on her a heartbeat more, then reholstered it. St. Augustina backed Papaqui up as paramedics appeared to take St. Dominic away. To their credit, the paramedics didn't flinch at the vomit. Another paramedic was over with Morlock, who sat a few feet away, breathing into a paper bag as he answered questions with nods and headshakes.

"I want her placed in handcuffs," the judge ordered, interrupting St. Augustina's assessment of the room.

"Your Honor—"

"Humor me," Judge Cartwright said, "I understand that the Magic Guild Guard have the ... *asset* under control, but she is still a dangerous thing, and I want her as secure as possible."

"It's alright," Papaqui said, touching St. Augustina's shoulder and then offering her hands in the universal "lock me up" gesture. St. Augustina retrieved a pair of cuffs from the court officer and placed them on her, pocketing the key.

The judge did not resume her seat but was instead talking to a few other people who were both urgently freaked out.

One of them kept passing glances at Papaqui. Finally, the judge nodded, before rapping her gavel again. "I am adjourning this hearing for the time being. We will reschedule for a later date. We will be holding St. Dominick in contempt of court, assault, and attempted assault charges; all other decisions are on hold until a later date." Then she banged the gavel with a disgusted single pound. She left the room shortly after that.

St. Dominick did not return to consciousness by the time he was loaded up on a gurney and handcuffed to it. St. Augustina had no doubt he would not be seeing the inside of a jail cell any time soon, but either way, he was a serious piece taken off the board. Keeping her hand on Papaqui, she escorted her over to where Morlock still sat, working on breathing while a paramedic worked on wrapping up his arm enough to transport him. He was sternly looking away, taking a hit from his flask before the other paramedic caught him and confiscated it.

"The anti-nausea meds will work just fine," they snapped and tucked it into a pocket.

As the Saint approached, he looked up at her, his eyes completely black.

"Well, that was exciting," he murmured, giving her a weak smile.

"Are you alright?" St. Augustina asked, her eyes taking in his bleached-out face, her augments reporting that he was, in fact, not alright.

"I'll live, but they're going to probably have to knock me out to work on my arm. They wanted to give me blood, and I about passed out for them." He indicated a silver packet of the red stuff in one paramedic's hand, the outside label reading "for vampire emergency use only" in official-looking black letters. "Oh, the joys of being me."

"I'm sorry, Morlock," Papaqui said, her crest pulsing in agitation. Her officer's cap had been lost in the scuffle.

Morlock pinned her with his black stare. "Hey, look at me. This is not your fault," he emphasized. "It took me some time to come around to it, but Lady Ursula is right. You are a victim here, and it was my privilege to be the one to save you. Makes me a hero now, doesn't it?"

Papaqui's crest perked and stayed up at that encouragement.

"Buck up everyone. We won, more or less, eventually," Morlock crowed weakly.

"You think so?" Papaqui asked.

Morlock nodded, but St. Augustina was the one who answered. "St. Dominic's attack proved that Boyd is not safe in Paladin's custody. It was a calculated risk but a bad one. One I don't think St. Dominic would have taken without orders, so someone somewhere panicked." And there was a strong possibility that someone had been trying to cover their tracks and/ or protect their potential monopoly. There was still a good chance Boyd would have turned up dead in custody, which would snowball into other problems for their mysterious enemy, but it was something out of St. Augustina's control at the moment. None of this she could say out loud, but they had discussed all these possibilities prior to the hearing. She only had to meet Morlock's eyes for both of them to communicate the rest.

Morlock only added. "Boyd will be remanded to Magic Guild custody, and then things go from there."

"Okay, we're ready to move him," the first paramedic reported, and they both came around Morlock to help him to his feet. "We're going to move you now to the gurney—"

"I'd rather walk under my own power," Morlock stated.

"We don't advise that—" the other tried to say, but Morlock shook his head.

"I'll make it. I'm a hero. Let me have some scrap of my dignity."

The paramedics relented. He gave St. Augustina a triumphant smile and added, "I'll call you soon."

Once he left, St. Augustina returned to the court officer. "I am removing my ... 'evidence' back to the Magic Guild," she reported. He nodded and had her sign a few papers, and then

Papaqui and she walked out into the hall. There were still the dregs of commotion playing out in the hallway, but more people were more focused on their own cases and business, moving past without taking notice.

St. Augustina steered Papaqui down the hall, helping keep her steady in the press of bodies with her still in cuffs as they made their way to the Magic Guild transport door. There was a line, but she skipped it, coming to the front where the designated Opener stood, monitoring the door, since it wasn't a dedicated one to the Magic Guild.

"One moment, Constable," the attendant said, recognizing her and already pulling out a key from a neat ring of identical keys. "We have to wait for the door to clear, then you can go through."

St. Augustina nodded her understanding, and any grumbling from the line immediately quieted when they heard the attendant state her title. She could feel them staring but chose not to engage. They just needed to get through the door.

"Constable St. Augustina?" a voice asked from behind her.

She turned to regard a court page in a neat suit jacket and hair locked in place with too much gel.

"Yes?" she asked.

"Judge Alvarez-Hughes would like a moment to speak to you," he reported.

St. Augustina glanced at Papaqui, who gave a tiny shrug. The Saint nodded and the page led them through the halls again.

When they came to Judge Alvarez-Hughes's door, the page knocked twice and then opened it at the same time the gruff judge's voice bellowed, "Come in."

Nothing had changed in the judge's chambers except now he had a visitor.

"My lady?" St. Augustina asked, as Lady Ursula turned in her seat before the judge.

"Oh good, you brought poor Papaqui with you," Lady Ursula said, indicating the chair beside her. The page responded by grabbing up a third chair waiting against the wall and placing it on the other side of the empty one, then promptly left.

"Have a seat, Constable," the judge invited, not cordially, but not hostile either, so it was hard to get a read on what St. Augustina might expect from this conversation.

The Saint did as bid, but Papaqui still hesitated. The judge shifted uncomfortably in his seat as he took her in.

Luckily, Lady Ursula took point. "Papaqui, *please* have a seat. I have explained to the judge your circumstances."

The vampire coatl nodded, then complied, resting her cuffed hands on her lap. "I see."

"My God, it's uncanny," Judge Alvarez-Hughes said, leaning forward to rest his folded hands on his desk. "It is like you said, she's conscious."

"Papaqui?" Lady Ursula asked poignantly, refusing to speak about Papaqui as if she wasn't a person. She never had in the past month of working with her.

Papaqui cleared her throat. "As far as we know, I seem to be perfectly fine and ... normal, until I start to run out of energy that the spell animating me requires. Then I need a living blood infusion to return to this state of ... normal."

The judge nodded. "I have been a magic-sanctioned judge for thirteen years now, and I have never heard of a case like this," he marveled. "And she— you are bound to obey your master?"

Papaqui nodded. "Seems like."

"I think it is very clear why we need this emergency request granted under the Dangerous Magic Provisions Act," Lady Ursula said as the judge sat back in his chair, still trying to take it in.

"Of course," he agreed. "The implications should someone else gain control of such an ability... You are going to want to bring this before the Federal Magic oversight panel, but I don't see any problems getting this approved."

"Excellent, we simply want to continue to study the effects of this curse, and we are working on counter-spells and detection magics."

The judge nodded and proceeded to sign a series of documents, which he then folded and placed one copy in an envelope that he gave to Lady Ursula. "I'll file this personally."

"Thank you," Lady Ursula stood, slipping the envelope into a muff she had resting on her lap. "Come, Constable."

They stood along with the Judge. He and the Lady touched hands and then she exited. St. Augustina followed, only nodding to the judge as she led Papaqui out.

CHAPTER 25

"Was that necessary?" St. Augustina asked once they were safely back in the Magic Guild Guard offices.

"Yes, of course," Lady Ursula said, but St. Augustina shook her head.

"I don't mean the judge's order, I mean dragging me and Papaqui into the office."

"He needed to see proof before he would sign it, and she was with you, so yes," Lady Ursula replied, leaning forward to pick up her teacup from the set Papaqui had laid out for them when they had gotten back.

Irritated, St. Augustina picked up the hazelnut creamer from the tray and poured a good measure into the bitter black tea that Lady Ursula preferred at that moment.

Papaqui sat down beside St. Augustina, as she watched the two living women make up their cups.

"I'm just glad it's over," Papaqui said. "I really thought I was going to die. Again."

"We prepared for this. And we got lucky. He didn't manage to cut your head off, which would have been quite the headline," St. Augustina stated, gulping down a good measure of her dressed up tea before making up another cup.

Papaqui took a deep breath in. "And that means, it's over for me."

There was a heavy *tick tick tick* for a moment, then St. Augustina pulled out a third cup, pouring tea into it before handing it to Papaqui. The coatl hesitated then wrapped her scaled fingers around it, letting the warmth sink in. When she sipped it, a warm, humming trill slipped out as a smile forced its way on her face.

Papaqui swallowed. "It still tastes good, even if it does nothing for me."

St. Augustina pulled a fourth cup and poured another, then plucked up a creamer and sugar pack as she stood. "My thoughts exactly."

She went toward the door and, with a toe, slid over a small step stool to underneath the grotesque's perch.

"Now that the trial's over, I'd like to discuss what we do with our 'evidence.'" She stepped up on the stool with her cybernetically enhanced balance and slid the cup with its cream and sugar onto the grotesque's pedestal. "We didn't want to tell you this until we knew how things would turn out, but Lady Ursula has gotten consent from the Inner Council after showing them our findings from studying you for the last month, to release you indefinitely into my custody."

She turned to take in Papaqui's reaction and was met with Lady Ursula raising an eyebrow at her. "Am I speaking out of turn?" St. Augustina asked.

"Uh, no. No, not at all," Lady Ursula said, glancing at the grotesque. "You do know that not everything in the Magic Guild is a sentient creature, correct?"

St. Augustina glanced up at the watcher above, then back to her boss. "I'm taking the approach to best cover all bases."

"Fair enough," Lady Ursula stated then turned to Papaqui. "Yes, what the constable says is correct. It has been decided that the best place for you for the time being is in the constable's care."

Papaqui's crest pulsed as her tongue slipped out in time with it, the coatl equivalent of furrowed brows. "So... I'm not going to be destroyed?"

Lady Ursula shook her head with a gentle, "No, child."

"You're going to stay with me in my apartment and be under my care. I've got a spare room that I was going to turn into an office, but I really don't need it, so it is yours. What that means is these..." she pulled out Papaqui's coin necklace and held up the ring on her own finger that the medallion had been "slaved" to, "need to become permanent. If you consent."

Papaqui took her medallion back, looking down on it. "Permanent how?"

"We would like to insert that into your body somewhere, so that no matter what happens, you can't lose it or have it taken from you easily," Lady Ursula said. "It would still be bound to St. Augustina's ring."

"So I would obey her instead of Boyd again?" Papaqui supplied.

Lady Ursula nodded. "Yes. We weren't sure in the beginning if it would work, but so far, it seems our mixing magics has succeeded just fine. He no longer has any power over you."

"It's your choice if you want this or not," St. Augustina emphasized.

"But ... you want to?" Papaqui asked, looking up from her study of the medallion.

The Saint nodded. "Yes, I'm fine with it. And it's not just going to be you, Papaqui. I'm going to have a corresponding one inserted into my body as well."

That surprised both females in the room. "What? You don't have to do that?"

But St. Augustina held up a hand. "You may not be able to live the life you had before, but I will be damned if anyone else

is going to take your new one from you. Besides, I have enough hardware inside me as it is. What's one more augment? And your orders will remain the same. You act as you would as if you were still alive. Nothing else for you has to change."

"If that is what you both wish, it can be done," Lady Ursula conceded.

Papaqui covered her face with her hands.

The Saint and the lady exchanged concerned glances. "Papaqui?" St. Augustina prodded gently.

"Thank you, thank you," the coatl said, shaking her head as she was overcome with emotions. "I thought... I was so sure..." She uncovered her face as big, wet tears rolled down her face. "I kept telling myself that I was prepared... that I was ready to die, that I there was nothing I could do, but I never thought."

She moved to hide her face again, but Lady Ursula stopped her with an embrace, pulling the overwrought creature into a gentle hold as she hummed her version of crying.

Lady Ursula gave her a small nod over Papaqui's shoulder, a knowing smile of her own.

It was a win. Not the win she thought she would get when the Saint had started this case, but a win all the same.

This is justice, she thought. She hoped her mother would be proud. *I should give her a call. Things aren't going to be as busy now.*

Before she could finish that thought, however, the door to the Magic Guild Guard offices opened and a group of people walked in.

They stopped as St. Augustina spun around to face them. "Can I help you?"

They stared at her, all wearing matching uniforms with matching cautious expressions. A couple of glances went to Papaqui, who was trying to stop reptile-crying behind her.

Then St. Augustina's augmentations popped up a list of identities in her periphery. It was the rest of the guards that had walked out on her that first day.

The coatl stood up and came up beside the Saint.

"Hey, guys, what are you doing here?" she asked, as she readjusted her crest. Then spoke softly to St. Augustina. "Look, everyone came back."

"I see that," the constable said matching her tone. "Why?"

Another being, this one mostly hominal except for the fact that her hair was made of flowers and leaves, stepped up. She adjusted her turquoise shirt, which contrasted horribly with her skin color. "We've come to help," she said, her voice breathy and musical, as if her voice were made by the wind dancing through a tree. "We're reporting for duty."

"Oh" was all Papaqui said, then looked to St. Augustina for a reaction.

"If you'll have us," another officer, Montgomery added.

Around her, the other former officers were nodding their heads in agreement with the pronouncement.

Floored, the Saint looked back over her shoulder at Lady Ursula, who gestured with a wave of her hand. "It is your department."

"Yeah, it is," St. Augustina agreed, and she turned back to the group. She looked over all of them standing there in turn, waiting for her judgement. "*Sergeant* Papaqui..."

She turned to the coatl beside her, who didn't react at first, then jumped to attention. "Oh, uh, yes? Constable?"

"Let's get everyone here organized with half-hour time slots. We're apparently doing interviews today."

A few in the group started to cheer, while the rest of the faces became more somber, which made the cheerer's enthusiasm die as they tried to figure out what was going on.

"Uh, okay," Sergeant Papaqui said. She stepped up to the group as St. Augustina stepped back, leaving it to her to organize it all.

Lady Ursula rose as she approached. "Well, I should get out of your way. Looks like you have a busy rest of your day."

"Did you call them?" St. Augustina asked, pitching her voice down low.

A look of innocence draped over the Lady Wizardress's face. "Word about your work on behalf of the Magic Guild has reached many ears in our community. I think you will be having more than enough work to fill the entire room soon."

And with that, she flitted away out the door, leaving St. Augustina with a new passel of problems.

"Constable? Do you want everyone to have resumes?" Papaqui asked, recapturing her attention.

"Yes, if you can. Everyone is going to be assessed fresh. This is a new department."

"Yes, Constable," the room responded in chorus.

Already several of the potential recruits were moving the desks back into a semblance of formation throughout the room. A few more were handing out paper and pens and St. Augustina realized they were going to write out their resumes by hand. "Just include everything that you've been doing since you left the Magic Guild. I already have your previous records on file," she declared to the room, which apparently pleased the dryad to no end. Leaving them all to get ready, St. Augustina finally escaped to her office.

"Ma'am, ma'am, a moment please," Papaqui said, following her into the office.

"Yes, Sergeant?" the constable asked.

"St. Aug... ma'am," Papaqui fumbled, then she pitched her voice down low. "It's just. Sergeant? Really? There are more senior officers in this group than me."

"And you're the only one who stuck around, which means they passed on that chance for a promotion."

"Yeah, but ... that was Boyd."

St. Augustina set a hand on Papaqui's shoulder. "I need someone I can trust right now in this position."

"But I haven't even taken my sergeant's exam yet!"

"Which is why you are technically *acting* sergeant. I won't make it official until you do take the exam and pass it. Any more objections?"

Acting Sergeant Papaqui stood there, looking like she was trying to find one, but it just wasn't forthcoming.

St. Augustina sighed. "Papaqui, what is the real problem?"

"It's just... I don't know what to do?" she said softly.

"Make me a schedule for interviews for today and tomorrow and dismiss everyone who's coming tomorrow. Then we'll figure out the rest. Okay?"

Papaqui pursed her lips as her crest rose. She nodded with conviction. "Okay."

Then she turned and exited the office, barking with a larger voice than St. Augustina had ever heard come from the small being before. "Alright people, we're not going to get to all of you today, so who can stay and who can come back tomorrow?"

The office was alive again as the guards moved about the room. Through the closing door, St. Augustina could see Acting Sergeant Papaqui stop to answer questions, then gestured the first applicant toward the constable's office just as the wood door snickered closed only to pop open again.

"Constable? I'm the first up, can 1 come in?" asked Montgomery.

St. Augustina smiled and adjusted her badge. "Yes. The constable will see you now."

CHECK OUT ANOTHER BOOK IN
THE LUCKY DEVIL WORLD

https://a.co/d/dNpfHVg

When a charming and deadly corporate cyber-spy, shows up on the doorstep of Rune Leveau's bar, he wants only one thing: For the secretive Finder of the Lucky Devil to use her magical talent to find a wanted criminal. This criminal is the key to something very special... she can lead him to a computer program rumored to do the impossible: cast magic spells.

But Rune has a dangerous secret. She IS Anna Masterson. And despite the attraction between them, she refuses St. Benedict. If her secret gets discovered, she could lose everything again, even her life. The cyber-spy isn't going to take no for an answer. Not with his long-sought prize so close.

Join this continuing cyberpunk/urban fantasy sensation,
started in The Finder of the Lucky Devil.

DISCUSSION
QUESTIONS

1. Do you think Lady Ursula was right to push St. Augustina to take the case or not?

2. Was it a good idea to let Officer Papaqui back into the office so soon after she quit?

3. How did the treatment of the vampires in this society make you feel?

4. Why do you think the Paladin Police refused to hand the case over the Magic Guild?

5. Should St. Augustina have stuck to firing Papaqui when she tried?

6. What do you think is going on with the grotesque?

7. Even though Boyd is allegedly guilty, should Morlock still represent him?

8. Should the false vampire have been destroyed at the end? Why or why not?

9. Where do you think the story is going to go after the end?

10. What does justice mean to you?

AUTHOR BIO

Beyond the smashing success of her inaugural, Amazon bestseller, *The Finder of the Lucky Devil*, Megan Mackie is the author of The Lucky Devil Series (urban fantasy/cyberpunk), the Dead World Series (Post Post Zombie Apocalypse), *The Adventures of Pavlov's Dog and Schrodinger's Cat* (Midgrade science fiction) and the Working Mask series (wannabe superhero).

Her other work can be found on the Yonder app, where she has published three web novels, *Cookbooks and Demons* (paranormal demon romance), *Star Courier* (speculative Firefly-like fiction), and *Novantis* (steampunk political intrigue with sky pirates—think Bridgerton meets Black Sails). Outside of her own series, she is a contributing writer for the RPGs *Legendlore and Legendlore: Legacies* by Onyx Path Publishing and *Sirens: Battle of the Bards* through Apotheosis Studios.

When she isn't writing, she likes to play games—board games, puzzle boxes, RPGs, and video games. She lives in

Chicago with her husband and children, two dogs, two cats, and her mother in the apartment upstairs. She also has a thing for iconic leather hats.

Whats the news, Barman?

Sign Up for Megan's Newsletter!

https://www.meganmackieauthor.com/newsletter

Also check out her free Wattpad novel!

https://www.wattpad.com/1423396171-i-can%27t-get-the-vampire-rogue-to-romance-me

**It was all fun, until she got
sucked into the game.**

OTHER BOOKS BY MEGAN MACKIE

URBAN FANTASY/CYBERPUNK

THE LUCKY DEVIL SERIES
The Finder of the Lucky Devil
The Saint of Liars
The Devil's Day
The Digital Mage
Demonic Inc. – Coming Soon

THE SAINT CODE SERIES
The Lost
Constable – Coming Soon

MID-GRADE SCIENCE FICTION

THE ADVENTURES OF PAVLOV'S DOG AND SCHRODINGER'S CAT
Maxwell's Demon
The Ship of Theseus - Coming Soon
Sniffy the Virtual Rat – Coming Soon

POST POST-ZOMBIE APOCALYPSE

DEAD WORLD
The Prisoner of the Dead
The Journey to Naraka – Coming Soon
The Damned Road – Coming Soon

SUPERHERO

WORKING MASKS
The Vilification of Aqua Marine
The Indemnification of Black Heart - Coming Soon

EPIC FANTASY

SILVERBLOOD SERIES
Silverblood Scion